A VERY LONG ENGAG
"A kind of latter-day *War*
—*Los Angeles Book Review*

"A classic mystery. . . . Only the best historical fiction
can make the journey into a distant time and return with a
believable sense of how things really were."
—*Washington Post Book World*

ONE DEADLY SUMMER

"A rich and resonant sonata in black . . . the taut shaping
of a grand master!" —*Kirkus Reviews*

THE SLEEPING-CAR MURDERS

"The most welcome talent in the detective story to reach
us from France." —*New York Times*

THE LADY IN THE CAR
WITH GLASSES AND A GUN

"A chilling, baffling psychological fooler . . . sparkles with
all the juicy terror that can attack the heart and body."
—*Newsweek*

SÉBASITEN JAPRISOT is the author of the international bestseller
A Very Long Engagement. Trap for Cinderella is one of four noir
mysteries by Japrisot in a series that includes *The Lady in the
Car With Glasses and a Gun, The Sleeping-Car Murders,* and
One Deadly Summer, all published by Plume. A novelist,
screenwriter, and director, Japrisot lives in Marseilles, France.

TRAP FOR CINDERELLA

Sébastien Japrisot

TRANSLATED FROM THE FRENCH BY
HELEN WEAVER

A PLUME BOOK

PLUME
Published by the Penguin Group
Penguin Putnam Inc., 375 Hudson Street,
New York, New York 10014, U.S.A.
Penguin Books Ltd, 27 Wrights Lane, London W8 5TZ, England
Penguin Books Australia Ltd, Ringwood, Victoria, Australia
Penguin Books Canada Ltd, 10 Alcorn Avenue,
Toronto, Ontario, Canada M4V 3B2
Penguin Books (N.Z.) Ltd, 182–190 Wairau Road,
Auckland 10, New Zealand

Penguin Books Ltd, Registered Offices:
Harmondsworth, Middlesex, England

Published by Plume, an imprint of Dutton Signet,
a member of Penguin Putnam Inc.
Previously published by Simon and Schuster, Inc.

First Plume Printing, September, 1997
10 9 8 7 6 5 4 3 2 1

 REGISTERED TRADEMARK—MARCA REGISTRADA

LIBRARY OF CONGRESS CATALOGING-IN-PUBLICATION DATA
Japrisot, Sébastien
    [Piège pour Cendrillon, English]
    Trap for Cinderella / Sébastien Japrisot : translated from the
French by Helen Weaver.
        p.   cm.
    ISBN 0-452-27779-5
    I. Weaver, Helen.   II. Title.
PQ2678.O72P513   1997
843'.914—dc21   97–15740
                                                 CIP

Printed in the United States of America

PUBLISHER'S NOTE
This is a work of fiction. Names, characters, places, and incidents
either are the products of the author's imagination or are used
fictitiously, and any resemblance to actual persons, living or dead,
events, or locales are entirely coincidental.

TRAP FOR CINDERELLA

Amnesia:
- loss of memory
- mystery of the past
- rediscovery/re-invention
- confusion + forgotten info.
- has to/wants to believe people.
  Distorted info.

Mystery:
- large unknown that you need
  to narrow down.
- a bad guy, a crime, a good guy +
  a solution.
- investigation

I MURDERED

SUDDENLY THERE IS a great burst of white light, blinding me. Someone leans over me, a voice stabs my head, I hear screams echoing in distant corridors, but I know they are mine. I breathe in blackness through my mouth, a blackness peopled with strange faces, with murmurs, and I die again, happy.

A moment later—a day, a week, a year—the light returns on the other side of my eyelids, my hands burn, and my mouth, and my eyes. I am rolled down empty passageways, I scream again, and it is black.

Sometimes the pain is concentrated in a single spot behind my head. Sometimes I am aware of being moved, of being rolled elsewhere, and the pain spreads through my veins like a tongue of flame drying up my blood. In the blackness there is often fire, there is often water, but

7

I no longer suffer. The sheets of flame frighten me. The columns of water are cold and sweet to my sleep. I want the faces to fade away, the murmurs to die down. When I breathe in blackness through my mouth, I want the blackest black, I want to sink as deep as possible into the icy water, and never to come up.

Suddenly I come up, dragged toward the pain by my whole body, nailed by my eyes under the white light. I struggle, I howl, I hear my screams from a great distance, the voice that stabs my head brutally says things I do not understand.

Black. Faces. Murmurs. I feel good. *My child, if you start that again, I'll slap your face, with papa's fingers which are stained from cigarettes. Light papa's cigarette, angel, the fire, blow out the match, the fire.*

White. Pain on the hands, on the mouth, in the eyes. *Don't move. Don't move, child. There, easy. This won't hurt. Oxygen. Easy. There, good girl, good girl.*

Black. A woman's face. Two times two is four, three times two is six, ruler blows on the fingers. We walk in line. *Open your mouth wide when you sing.* All the faces walk in two lines. Where is the nurse? *I don't want any whispering in class. We will go to the beach when the weather is fine. Is she talking? At first she was delirious. Since the graft she complains of her hands, but not her face.* The sea. If you go out too far, you will drown. *She complains of her mother, and of a schoolteacher who used to hit her on the fingers.* The waves went over my head. Water, my hair in the water, go under, come up again, light.

I came to the surface one morning in September, with lukewarm hands and face, lying on my back on clean sheets. There was a window near my bed, and a great splash of sunlight in front of me.

A man came and spoke to me in a very gentle voice, for a time which seemed to me too short. He told me to be a good girl, and not to try to move my head or hands. He cut off his syllables when he spoke. He was calm and reassuring. He had a long bony face and large black eyes. But his white gown hurt my eyes. He realized this when he saw me lower my eyelids.

The second time he came in a gray woolen jacket. He spoke to me again. He asked me to close my eyes for yes. I had pain, yes. In my head, yes. On my hands, yes. On my face, yes. I understood what he was saying, yes. He asked me whether I knew what had happened. He saw that I kept my eyes open, in despair.

He went away and my nurse came to give me an injection so I could sleep. She was tall, with large white hands. I realized that my face was not uncovered like hers. I made an attempt to feel the bandages, the salve, on my skin. Mentally I followed, piece by piece, the strip that wound around my neck, continued over the nape of my neck and the top of my head, wound around my forehead, missed my eyes, and wound once more around the lower part of my face, winding, winding. I fell asleep.

In the days that followed, I was someone who is moved around, fed, rolled through passageways, who answers by closing her eyes once for yes, twice for no, who tries not to scream, who howls when her dressings are changed, who tries to convey with her eyes the questions that oppress her, who can neither speak nor move, a creature whose body is cleansed with ointments, as her mind is with injections, a thing without hands or face: no one.

"Your bandages will be removed in two weeks," said the doctor with the bony face. "Frankly, I'll be a little sorry: I rather liked you as a mummy."

He had told me his name: Doulin. He was pleased that I was able to remember it five minutes later, and even more pleased to hear me pronounce it correctly. Before, when he used to hover over me, he would simply say *mademoiselle,* or *child,* or *good girl,* and I would repeat *mamaschool, goodiplication, mamarule,* words which my mind knew were wrong, but which my stiffened lips formed against my will. Later he called this "telescoping"; he said that it was the least of our worries and would disappear very quickly.

Actually it took me less than ten days to recognize verbs and adjectives when I heard them. Common nouns took me a few days more. I never recognized proper nouns. I was able to repeat them just as correctly as the others, but they recalled nothing besides what Dr. Doulin had told me. Except for a few like Paris, France, China, Place Masséna or Napoleon, they remained locked in a past which was unknown to me. I relearned them, but that was all. It was pointless, however, to explain to me what was meant by to eat, to walk, bus, skull, clinic, or anything that was not a definite person, place, or event. Dr. Doulin said this was normal, and I was not to worry about it.

"Do you remember my name?"

"I remember everything you've said. When can I see myself?"

He moved away, and when I tried to follow him with my eyes it hurt. He returned with a mirror. I looked at myself, me: two eyes and a mouth in a long, hard helmet swathed in gauze and white bandages.

"It takes over an hour to undo all that. What's underneath should be very pretty."

He was holding the mirror in front of me. I was leaning back against a pillow, almost sitting up, my arms tied to the bed at my sides.

"Are they going to untie my hands?"

"Soon. You'll have to be good and not move around too much. They'll be fastened only at night."

"I see my eyes. They're blue."

"Yes, they're blue. You're going to be good now: not move, not think, just sleep. I'll be back this afternoon."

The mirror vanished, and that thing with blue eyes and a mouth. The long bony face reappeared.

"Sleep tight, little mummy."

I felt myself slipping into a lying position. I wished I could see the doctor's hands. Faces, hands, eyes were all that mattered just then. But he was gone, and I went to sleep without an injection, tired all over, repeating a name which was as unfamiliar as the rest: my own.

"Michele Isola. They call me Mi, or Micky. I am twenty years old. I'll be twenty-one in November. I was born in Nice. My father still lives there."

"Easy, Mummy. You're swallowing half your words and wearing yourself out."

"I remember everything you've said. I lived several years in Italy with my aunt who died in June. I was burned in a fire about three months ago."

"What else did I tell you?"

"I had a car. Make, MG. Registration number, TTX 664313. Color, white."

"Very good, Mummy."

I tried to reach out to keep him from going, and a

stab of pain shot up my arm to the nape of my neck. He never stayed more than a few minutes. Then they gave me something to drink, they put me to sleep.

"My car was white. Make, MG. Registration number, TTX 664313."

"The house?"

"It's on a promontory called Cap Cadet, between La Ciotat and Bandol. It had two stories, three rooms and a kitchen below, three rooms and two bathrooms above."

"Not so fast. Your room?"

"It overlooked the sea and a town called Les Lecques. The walls were painted blue and white. This is ridiculous: I remember everything you say."

"It's important, Mummy."

"What's important is that I'm repeating. It doesn't mean anything. They're just words."

"Could you repeat them in Italian?"

"No. I remember *camera, casa, machina, bianca*. I've already told you that."

"That's enough for today. When you're better, I'll show you some photographs. I have three big boxes of them. I know you better than you know yourself, Mummy."

It was a doctor named Chaveres who had operated on me, three days after the fire, in a hospital in Nice. Dr. Doulin said that his operation, after two hemorrhages in the same day, had been wonderful to watch and full of amazing details, but that he wouldn't want any surgeon to have to repeat it.

I was in a clinic in Boulogne * run by a Dr. Dinne. I

* A section on the outskirts of Paris, just south of the Bois de Boulogne. ——*Translator.*

12

had been moved there a month after the first operation. I had had a third hemorrhage in the plane when the pilot had been forced to increase altitude a quarter of an hour before landing.

"Dr. Dinne took charge of you as soon as the graft had passed the critical stage. He made you a pretty nose. I've seen the plaster cast. It's very pretty, I assure you."

"What about you?"

"I am Dr. Chaveres' brother-in-law. I work at Saint Anne's. I've been looking after you from the day you were brought to Paris."

"What have they done to me?"

"Here? They've made you a pretty nose, Mummy."

"But before that?"

"That doesn't matter now; what matters is you're here. You're lucky to be twenty years old."

"Why can't I see anyone? If I saw someone, my father, or anyone I knew, I'm sure everything would come back to me in one blow."

"You have a way with words, my dear. You've already had one blow on the head which gave us enough trouble. The fewer you have now, the better."

Smiling, he moved his hand slowly toward my shoulder and let it rest there a moment without pressure.

"Don't worry, Mummy. Everything is going to be fine. In a while your memory will come back a little at a time, without a fuss. There are many kinds of amnesia, almost as many as there are amnesics. But you have a very nice kind: retrograde, lacunary, no aphasia, not even a stammer, and so comprehensive, so complete, that now the gap can only get smaller. So it's a tiny, tiny little thing."

He held out his thumb and index finger, almost touching, for me to see. He smiled and rose with deliberate slowness, so that I would not have to move my eyes too abruptly.

"Be good, Mummy."

The time came when I was so good that they no longer knocked me out three times a day with a pill in my broth. This was in late September, nearly three months after the accident. I could pretend to be asleep and let my memory beat its wings against the bars of its cage.

There were sun-filled streets, palm trees by the sea, a school, a classroom, a teacher with her hair pulled back, a red wool bathing suit, nights illuminated by Chinese lanterns, military bands, being offered chocolate by an American soldier—and the gap.

Afterward, there was a sudden burst of white light, the nurse's hands, Dr. Doulin's face.

Sometimes I saw again very clearly, with a harsh and disturbing clarity, a pair of thick butcher's hands with large but nimble fingers and the face of a stout man with cropped hair. These were the hands and face of Dr. Chaveres glimpsed between two blackouts, two comas, a memory which I placed in the month of July, when he had brought me into that white, indifferent, incomprehensible world.

I did mental calculations, the back of my neck painful against the pillow, my eyes closed. I saw these calculations being written on a blackboard. I was twenty. According to Dr. Doulin, the American soldiers were giving chocolate to little girls in 1944 or '45. My memories did not go beyond five or six years after my birth: fifteen years wiped out.

I concentrated on proper names, because these were the words that evoked nothing, were connected with nothing in this new life I was being forced to live. Georges Isola, my father; Firenze, Roma, Napoli; Les Lecques, Cap Cadet. It was useless, and later I learned from Dr. Doulin that I was beating my head against a wall.

"I told you not to disturb yourself, Mummy. If your father's name reminds you of nothing, it is because you've forgotten your father with the rest. His name doesn't matter."

"But when I say the word river, or fox, I know what it means. Have I seen a river or a fox since the accident?"

"Look, sweet, when you're yourself again, I promise you we'll have a long talk about it. Meanwhile I would rather you remained quiet. Just tell yourself you're going through a process which is definite, understood, one might almost say, normal. Every morning I see ten old men who haven't been hit on the head and who are in almost exactly the same state. Five or six years is just about the age limit of their memories. They remember their schoolteacher, but not their children or grand-children. This doesn't prevent them from playing their *belote*. They have forgotten almost everything, but not *belote* or how to roll their cigarettes. That's the way it is. You've got us stymied with an amnesia of a senile variety. If you were a hundred, I'd tell you to take care of yourself and that would be that. But you're twenty. There's not one chance in a million that you will stay like this. Do you understand?"

"When can I see my father?"

"Soon. In a few days they'll take off this medieval con-traption you have on your face. After that, we'll see."

"I want to know what happened."

"Another time, Mummy. There are things I want to

15

be very sure of, and if I stay too long, you'll get tired. Now, what's the number of the MG?"

"664313 TTX."

"Are you purposely saying it backward?"

"Yes, I am! I can't stand it! I want to move my hands! I want to see my father! I want to get out of here! You make me say the same stupid things over and over every day! I can't stand it!"

"Easy, Mummy."

"Stop calling me that!"

"Calm yourself, please."

I lifted one arm, an enormous plaster fist. This was the afternoon of "the fit." The nurse came. They retied my hands. Dr. Doulin stood against the wall opposite me and stared at me with eyes full of shame and resentment.

I howled, no longer knowing whether it was him or myself I hated. I was given an injection. I saw other nurses and doctors come into the room. I believe it was the first time that I actually thought about my physical appearance. I had the sensation of seeing myself through the eyes of those who were watching me, as if I were two people in this white room, this white bed. A formless thing, with three holes, ugly, shameful, howling. I howled with horror.

Dr. Dinne came to see me in the days that followed, and talked to me as if I were a five-year-old girl, a little spoiled, something of a nuisance, who had to be protected from herself.

"If you start that performance again, I won't be responsible for what we'll find under your bandages. You'll have only yourself to blame."

Dr. Doulin did not come back for a whole week. It was I who had to ask, several times, for him. My nurse, who must have been criticized after "the fit," answered my questions reluctantly. She untied my arms for two hours a day, during which time she kept her eyes fastened on me, suspicious and ill at ease.

"Are you the one who stays with me while I sleep?"

"No."

"Who's that?"

"Someone else."

"I'd like to see my father."

"You're not ready to."

"I'd like to see Dr. Doulin."

"Dr. Dinne does not wish it."

"Tell me something."

"What?"

"Anything. Talk to me."

"It's not allowed."

I looked at her large hands, which I found beautiful and reassuring. Eventually she became aware of my gaze and was annoyed by it.

"Stop watching me that way."

"You're the one that's watching me."

"You need to be watched," she said.

"How old are you?"

"Forty-six."

"How long have I been here?"

"Seven weeks."

"Have you taken care of me all that time?"

"Yes. That's enough, now."

"How was I at first?"

"You didn't move."

"Was I delirious?"

"Sometimes."

"What did I say?"

"Nothing of interest."

"What, though?"

"I can't remember now."

At the end of another week, another eternity, Dr. Doulin came into the room with a package under his arm. He was wearing a dirty raincoat which he did not remove. The rain beat against the window panes beside my bed.

He came over to me, touched my shoulder the way he always did, very quickly and gently, and said, "Hello, Mummy."

"I've waited a long time for you."

"I know," he said. "I got a present out of it."

He explained that someone outside the clinic had sent him flowers after "the fit." The bouquet—dahlias, because his wife liked them—was accompanied by a little key chain for the car. He showed it to me. It was a round object, in gold, which struck the hours. Very useful for parking in a time zone.

"Was it my father who sent the present?"

"No. Someone who has taken care of you since the death of your aunt, whom you have seen much more of than you have of your father in the last few years. It's a woman. Her name is Jeanne Murneau. She followed you to Paris. She asks after you three times a day."

I told him that this name meant nothing to me. He took a chair, set the timer on his key chain, and put it on the bed near my arm.

"In fifteen minutes it'll ring and I'll have to go. How do you feel, Mummy?"

"I wish you'd stop calling me that."

"After tomorrow I'll never call you that again. You'll be taken to the operating room in the morning. Your bandages will be removed. Dr. Dinne thinks everything should be nicely healed."

He unwrapped the package he had brought. It was photographs, photographs of me. He handed them to me one at a time, watching my eyes. He did not seem to expect me to recognize anything. At any rate, I did not. I saw a girl with black hair who looked very pretty, who smiled a great deal, who had a slender figure and long legs, who was sixteen in some of the pictures and eighteen in others.

The pictures were glossy, beautiful, and horrible to contemplate. I did not even try to remember this clear-eyed face, nor the series of landscapes I was shown. From the first photograph, I knew it would be wasted effort. I was happy, eager to look at myself and unhappier than I had been since I had opened my eyes under the white light. I felt like laughing and crying at once. In the end, I cried.

"There, there. Don't be silly."

He put the pictures away, in spite of my desire to see them again.

"Tomorrow I'll show you some others in which you are not alone, but with Jeanne Murneau, your aunt, your father, friends you had three months ago. You mustn't expect this to bring back your past. But it will help you."

I said yes, that I had confidence in him. The key chain rang near my arm.

I walked back from the operating room with the help of my nurse and an assistant of Dr. Dinne's: thirty steps along a corridor of which I saw only the tiled floor under the napkin that covered my head. A black and white checkerboard pattern. I was put back in bed, my arms more tired than my legs, because my hands were still in their heavy casts.

They arranged me in a sitting position with the pillow behind my back. Dr. Dinne, in a suit, joined us in the room. He seemed pleased. He watched me curiously, attentive to my every movement. My naked face felt cold as ice.

"May I see myself?"

He motioned to the nurse. He was a stout little man without much hair. The nurse came toward the bed with the mirror in which I had seen myself in my mask two weeks before.

My face, my eyes looking at my eyes: a short, straight nose. Skin taut over prominent cheekbones. Full lips opening in an anxious little smile, slightly plaintive. A color not ghastly, as I was expecting, but rosy, freshly scrubbed. In short, a very attractive face, which lacked naturalness because I still did not dare move the muscles beneath the skin, and which I found decidedly oriental because of the cheekbones and the eyes, which were drawn toward the temples. My face, immobile and mysterious, down which I saw two warm tears trickle, then two more, and two more. My own face, which was becoming blurred, which I could no longer see.

"Your hair will grow back fast," said the nurse. "Look how much it's grown in three months under the bandages. Your eyelashes will get longer too."

Her name was Mme. Raymonde. She did the best she could with my hair: there was three inches of it to hide

20

the scars, and she arranged it a lock at a time to give it body. She washed my face and neck with absorbent cotton. She smoothed my eyebrows. She seemed to have forgiven me for "the fit." She prepared me every day as if for a wedding.

She said, "You look like a little monk, or Joan of Arc. Do you know who Joan of Arc was?"

She had brought me from outside, as I had requested, a large mirror which was fastened to the foot of my bed. I stopped looking at myself only when I slept.

She was more willing to talk to me too, during the long hours of the afternoon. She would sit on a chair near me and knit or smoke a cigarette, so close that by bending my head slightly I could see both our faces in the mirror.

"Have you been a nurse for a long time?"

"Twenty-five years. I've been here for ten."

"Have you had patients like me before?"

"There are a lot of people who want their noses changed."

"I'm not talking about them."

"I took care of an amnesic once. A long time ago."

"Did she get well?"

"She was very old."

"Show me the pictures again."

She went and got from the dresser the box that Dr. Doulin had left with us. One by one she handed me pictures which had never meant anything to me, which no longer caused even the pleasure of those first moments when I thought I was on the verge of discovering the continuity behind these gestures frozen on glossy 9 x 12 paper.

I looked, for the twentieth time, at someone who had

been me, whom I already found less attractive than the girl with short hair at the foot of my bed.

I also looked at a stout woman with heavy jowls wearing a pince-nez. This was my Aunt Midola. She never smiled, she wore knitted shawls around her shoulders, and she was sitting down in all the pictures.

I looked at Jeanne Murneau, who had been devoted to my aunt for fifteen years, who had been with me constantly for the last six or seven years, who had come to live in Paris when I had been moved there from Nice after the operation. The graft, a piece of skin ten inches square—that was her. And also the flowers in my room, fresh every day, the nightgowns which I had to be content to admire, the cosmetics which were still forbidden, the bottles of champagne which were lined up against the wall, the candy which Mme. Raymonde distributed among her colleagues in the hall.

"Have you seen her?"

"That young woman? Yes, several times, around one o'clock when I go to lunch."

"What does she look like?"

"Like the pictures. You'll be able to see her in a few days."

"Has she spoken to you?"

"Yes, several times."

"What did she say?"

" 'Take good care of my little girl.' She was your aunt's right arm in a way, a sort of secretary or housekeeper. It was she who took care of you in Italy. Your aunt could hardly get around at the end."

In the photographs Jeanne Murneau was tall, serene, rather good-looking, rather well-dressed, rather severe. She was next to me in only one picture. It was in the snow. We were wearing fitted pants and wool caps with tassels. In spite of the tassels, the skis, and the smile on the face of the girl who was me, the picture did not give an impression of lightheartedness or friendship.

"She looks as if she's mad at me here."

Mme. Raymonde turned the print around to look at it, and nodded her head grimly.

"No doubt you gave her good reason. You got into more than one jam, you know."

"How do you know?"

"The papers."

"Oh."

The papers for July had told the story of the Cap Cadet fire. Dr. Doulin was keeping the issues that discussed me and the other girl, and still would not show them to me.

The other girl was also in the photographs. They were all there: tall, short, pretty, ugly, all unknown, all smiling the same set smile which I was tired of seeing.

"I've seen enough for today."

"Would you like me to read to you?"

"Yes, my father's letters."

There were three from him, a hundred from friends and relatives I no longer knew. Best wishes for a quick recovery. We live in anxiety. I no longer exist. I can't wait to hold you in my arms. Dear Mi. My Micky. Mi darling. My sweet. My poor child.

My father's letters were kind, worried, shy, and disappointing. There were two boys who had written me in Italian. Someone else, who signed himself Francois, declared that I would belong to him always, that he would make me forget this hell.

From Jeanne Murneau, however, there was only a

note, sent two days before the removal of my mask. It was delivered to me then with the letters. It must have come with a box of candied fruits or some silk underwear, or the little watch I was wearing on my wrist. It said, "My Mi, my love, my angel, you are not alone, I promise you. Don't worry. Don't be unhappy. Love and kisses, Jeanne."

I didn't have to have this one read to me; I knew it by heart.

They removed the casts and bandages that immobilized my arms. They put on a pair of soft, lightweight white cotton gloves without letting me see my hands.

"Will I have to wear gloves like this?"

"The main thing is that you have the use of your hands. The bones are not damaged, the knuckles will be painful only for a few days. You won't be able to fix watches with these fingers, but you will be able to make all the ordinary movements. At the worst, you'll have to give up playing tennis."

It was not Dr. Dinne who spoke, but one of the two doctors he had brought into the room. They were answering me severely for my own good, to keep me from feeling sorry for myself.

They made me bend and unbend my fingers for a few minutes, and open and close my hands on theirs. They left, giving me an appointment for a checkup X ray two weeks later.

It was the morning for doctors. After the two there came a cardiologist, then Dr. Doulin. I walked around the flower-filled room dressed in a skirt of thick blue wool and a white blouse. The cardiologist unbuttoned my blouse to listen to a heart which he pronounced sound. I thought about my hands which I would soon see without my gloves. I thought about my high-heeled shoes, which had immediately seemed natural to me. If everything had been wiped out, if I had somehow become a little girl of five, should not all these things—high-heeled shoes, stockings, lipstick—seem strange to me?

"You're impossible," said Dr. Doulin. "I've told you ten times not to go into ecstasies over this kind of nonsense. If I should invite you to dinner now, and you were to hold your fork properly, what would that prove? That your hands remember better than you do? Even if I let you take the wheel of my car, and after a little trouble with the gears because you're not used to a 403, you were to drive more or less normally, do you think we would have learned anything?"

"I don't know. You should explain it to me."

"I should also keep you a few days longer. Unfortunately, they're anxious to take you away. I have no legal power to keep you here, unless you want to stay. And I'm not even sure I'm right to ask it of you."

"Who wants to take me away?"

"Jeanne Murneau. She says she can't stand it any more."

"Am I going to see her?"

"What do you think all this packing is about?"

Without looking around, he indicated with his hand the room, the open door, Mme. Raymonde arranging my clothes, another nurse taking away the bottles of champagne and piles of books which had not been read to me.

"Why do you want me to stay?"

"You are leaving with a nice face, a little heart in good order, hands you will be able to use, a third left frontal convolution which gives every indication of being fit as a fiddle: I was hoping that when you left you would take away your memory as well."

"The third what?"

"Frontal convolution. The left side of the brain. That was where you had your first hemorrhage. The aphasia I noticed at first must have originated there. It has nothing to do with the rest."

"What is the cause of the rest?"

"I don't know. Perhaps simply the fear you must have experienced during the fire. Or the shock. While the house was on fire, you were thrown outside. You were found at the foot of a flight of stairs, with a head wound over four inches long. In any case, the amnesia from which you suffer is not related to any brain injury. I thought so at first, but it's something else."

I was sitting on my unmade bed, my white-gloved hands resting on my knees. I told him that I wanted to leave, that I couldn't stand it any more either, that when I saw Jeanne Murneau, when I talked to her, everything would come back to me.

He spread his hands in a gesture of resignation.

"She will be here this afternoon. She will certainly want to take you away immediately. If you stay in Paris I will see you at the hospital or at my office. If she takes you south, it is imperative that you see Dr. Chaveres."

He was sharp and I could see he was annoyed with me. I told him that I would come to see him often, but that I would go mad if I stayed in this room any longer.

"There is only one madness you have to worry about," he told me, "and that would be to think, 'I have plenty of time to make new memories.' Later you would be sorry."

He left me with this thought, which in fact had already occurred to me. Now that I had a face, the fifteen lost years did not bother me so much. All I had left was a tolerable pain in the back of the neck, a heaviness in the head, and that, too, would disappear. When I looked at myself in the mirror, I was myself, I had the face of a little monk, a life waiting for me outside, I was happy, I liked myself. Never mind the "other one," since this one was me.

"Do you know, when I see myself in this mirror I adore myself, I'm mad about myself!"

I was talking to Mme. Raymonde and pirouetting to make my skirt whirl. My legs were poor partners to my enthusiasm: I almost lost my balance and stopped in confusion: Jeanne was there.

She was standing in the doorway with one hand on the doorknob, her face strangely immobile, her hair lighter than I had imagined, in a beige outfit that caught the sun. Something else I had not noticed in her pictures was that she was very tall, almost a head taller than I.

Her face and manner were not really strange to me, and for a second I thought the past was going to rise up in one great wave and knock me down. It must have been the dizziness from turning around, or the unexpected presence of a woman who was as familiar to me as someone encountered in a dream. I fell onto my bed and instinctively I hid my face and hair in my gloved hands, as if I were ashamed of them.

A moment later Mme. Raymonde had discreetly left the room. I saw Jeanne's lips part, I heard her voice, which was soft, low, and intimate like her gaze, and then she came over to me and took me in her arms.

"Don't cry."

"I can't help it."

I kissed her cheek, her neck, I regretted that I could touch her only through my gloves, I even recognized her perfume, which also came from a dream. With my head against her breast, ashamed of my hair which she was brushing aside gently and which would surely reveal the scars, I told her that I was unhappy, that I wanted to go away with her, that she could not know how I had waited for her.

"Let me look at you."

I did not want to, but she made me raise my head, and her eyes, so close to mine, made me believe again that everything was going to come back to me. Her eyes were golden, very light, and something hesitant stirred in their depths.

She, too, was renewing her acquaintance. She studied me with a puzzled expression. Finally I could not bear this examination, this searching of my face for a girl who had disappeared. I took her by the wrists, crying harder than ever, and pushed her away from me.

"Take me away, please. Don't look at me. It's me, Mi! Don't look at me."

She continued to stroke my hair, calling me her darling, her baby, her angel. Then Dr. Dinne came in. He was embarrassed by my tears, and by the height of Jeanne who, when she got up, was taller than anyone else in the room: taller than he, or his assistants, or Mme. Raymonde.

There were instructions, a long exchange of anxieties in my behalf which I did not understand, which I no longer wanted to understand. I was standing huddled against Jeanne. She had her arm around me, she was speaking to them in the voice of a queen who was taking away her child, her Mi. I was happy, I was no longer afraid of anything.

It was she who buttoned my coat, a suede one I must have had on before, for it was worn at the sleeves. It was she who arranged a beret on my head and knotted a green silk scarf around my neck. It was she who guided me through the corridors of the clinic, toward a glass door splashed with sunlight, blinding.

Outside was a white car with a black top. She helped me into the seat, closed the door, and reappeared at the wheel. She was calm and silent, and from time to time she looked at me and smiled, or placed a quick kiss on my temple.

We were off. Gravel under the wheels; a gate opening; wide avenues with trees on either side.

"This is the Bois de Boulogne," said Jeanne.

I was tired. My eyelids were dropping. I felt myself slipping, my head lying on the velvety material of her skirt. Near my head I saw a piece of the steering wheel turn. I was miraculously alive. I fell asleep.

I awoke on a low couch with a red plaid blanket over my legs, in a huge room in which the light of the table lamps did not chase the shadows from every corner.

A fire was burning in a high fireplace thirty paces away, across the room. I got up, the weight of emptiness in my head heavier than ever. I walked over to the fire, drew a chair up to it, sank into it, and again fell into a light sleep.

Later I was aware that Jeanne was leaning over me. I heard her voice murmuring. Then suddenly I thought I remembered Godmother Midola being rolled in her wheel chair, her orange shawl over her shoulders, ugly, horrible. . . . I opened my eyes to a season that made my head swim, where everything was blurred as if seen through a rain-drenched glass.

The world came back into focus. Jeanne's clear face and golden hair were over me. I had the impression that she had been looking at me for a long time.

"How do you feel?"

I said I was fine, and held out my arms to her. Beyond her hair, which was against my cheek, I saw the enormous room, the paneled walls, the lamps, the shadowy corners, the couch I had abandoned. The blanket was around my knees.

"What is this place?"

"A house someone's letting me use. I'll explain later. Do you feel all right? You fell asleep in the car."

"I'm cold."

"I took off your coat. I shouldn't have. Just a minute."

She held me tighter, then rubbed my arms and back vigorously to warm me. I laughed. She drew back with an impenetrable expression, and again I saw hesitation in the depths of her eyes. Then, abruptly, she joined in my laughter. She handed me a cup which had been placed on the carpet.

"Drink it. It's tea."

"Did I sleep a long time?"

"Three hours. Drink."

"Are we alone here?"

"No. There's a cook and a butler who don't know what to make of you. Drink. They couldn't get over it when I brought you from the car. You're thinner. I carried you myself. I'm going to do everything I can to put some weight on you. When you were little you used to hate me for making you eat."

"I hated you?"

"Drink. No, you didn't hate me. You were thirteen. Your ribs stuck out. You have no idea how ashamed I was of those ribs. Drink, do you hear?"

I drank the tea in one swallow. It was lukewarm, and the taste was not unfamiliar, although I did not particularly like it.

"You don't like it?"

"Not especially, no."

"You used to, before."

From now on there would always be this "before." I told Jeanne that they had given me a little coffee my last days at the clinic, and that it was good for me. Jeanne bent over the chair and said that she would give me whatever I liked, the main thing was that I was here, alive.

"Just now, at the clinic, you didn't recognize me, did you?"

"Of course I recognized you."

"Did you?"

"You're my baby," she said. "The first time I saw you was at the airport in Rome. You were very small, with a huge suitcase. You had the same lost look. Your godmother told me, 'Murneau, if you don't fatten her up, you're fired.' I fed you, washed you, dressed you, taught you Italian, tennis, checkers, the Charleston, everything. I even gave you two spankings. From thirteen to eighteen, you never left me for more than three days at a time. You were my own girl. Your godmother used to say that you were my 'job.' And now I'm going to start all over again. If you don't become just as you were, I'll fire myself."

She listened to my laugh, studying me with such an intense look that I stopped abruptly.

31

"What's the matter?"

"Nothing, darling. Get up."

She took my arm and asked me to walk across the room, drawing back to observe me. I took a few halting steps, with a painful emptiness at the back of my neck and in my legs that felt like lead.

When she came back to me, I thought she was making an effort to hide her dismay so as not to increase my own. She managed to put on a confident smile, as if I had always looked like this: high cheekbones, short nose, cropped hair. Somewhere in the house a clock struck seven.

"Have I changed so much?" I asked her.

"Your face has changed. And then, you're tired, it's natural that your gestures and walk should not be the same. I'll have to get used to it myself."

"How did it happen?"

"Later, darling."

"I want to remember. You, me, Aunt Midola, my father, the others: I want to remember."

"You will remember."

"Why did we come here? Why don't you take me straight to some place I know, where they know me?"

She was not to answer this question until three days later. For the moment, she held me close, she rocked me in her arms, she called me her little girl, and said that they would not hurt me any more because she would never leave me again.

"Did you leave me?"

"Yes. A week before the accident. I had some business of your godmother's to settle in Nice. I returned to the villa to find you more dead than alive at the foot of a stairway. I went mad trying to find an ambulance, the police, a doctor.''

We were in another huge room, a dining room with somber furnishings and a table ten feet long. We were sitting next to each other. I had the plaid blanket over my shoulders.

"Had I been at Cap Cadet a long time?"

"Three weeks," she said. "I stayed there with the two of you for the first few days."

"The two of us?"

"You, and a girl you liked to be with. Eat. If you won't eat, I won't talk."

I swallowed pieces of steak to get pieces of the past. We played this game sitting side by side in a big, gloomy house in Neuilly, served by a cook who moved furtively and called Jeanne by her family name without saying mademoiselle or madame.

"The girl was one of your childhood friends," said Jeanne. "She had grown up in the same house with you in Nice. Her mother did your mother's laundry. You lost track of each other when you were eight or nine, but you ran into her again this year in February. She was working in Paris. You became attached to her. Her name was Domenica Loi."

Jeanne was watching me, waiting for a sign of recognition to appear on my face. But it was hopeless. She was talking about people whom I pitied, but who were strangers to me.

"Is that the girl who died?"

"Yes. She was found in the part of the villa that was burned. It looked as though you had tried to get her out of her room before you were burned. Your nightgown caught on fire. You must have been trying to get to the swimming pool—there's one in the garden. I found you at the foot of the stairs half an hour later. It was two o'clock in the morning. People had come running in their pajamas, but no one dared touch you, everyone was frantic, they didn't know what to do. The Les Lecques fire department arrived right after I did. They took you to the naval infirmary in La Ciotat. During the night I could have ordered an ambulance from Marseille, but in the end it was a helicopter that came. They took you to Nice. You were operated on the next day."

"What was the matter with me?"

"You must have fallen at the bottom of the stairs as you were rushing out of the house. Unless you decided to go out the window and let yourself fall from the second story. We learned nothing from the investigation. What we do know for sure is that you fell head first onto the steps. You were burned on the face and hands. Also on the body, but less seriously; the nightgown must have given you some protection. The firemen explained that to me, but I've forgotten. You were naked, black from head to foot, with shreds of charred cloth in your hands and mouth. You had no hair. The people I found with you thought you were dead. You had a cut on the top of your head as long as my hand. This was the injury we were most worried about the first night. Later, after Dr. Chaveres' operation, I signed a paper for a skin graft. Yours wouldn't heal any more."

She spoke without looking at me. Each sentence entered my head like a burning drill. She pushed her chair away from the table and pulled her skirt above her legs.

I saw a dark patch on her right thigh, above the stocking: the graft.

I put my head into my gloved hands and began to cry. Jeanne put her arm around my shoulder and we stayed this way for several minutes, until the cook came in and placed a tray of fruit on the table.

"I must tell you all this," said Jeanne. "You must know and remember."

"I know."

"You are here, nothing can happen to you. It's all over now."

"How did the fire start?"

She rose, her skirt fell back down. She went to a buffet and lit a cigarette. She held the match in front of her for a moment so I could see it.

"A gas leak in the girl's bedroom. Gas had been installed in the villa a few months before. The investigation concluded that there must have been a bad connection. The pilot light of the water heater in one of the bathrooms caused an explosion."

She blew out the match.

"Come here," I said.

She came over and sat down beside me. I put out my hand, took her cigarette, and inhaled a puff. I liked it.

"Did I smoke, before?"

"Get up," said Jeanne. "Let's look around. Bring an apple with you. Dry your eyes."

In a low-ceilinged room with a bed big enough for four of me in my present condition, Jeanne made me put on a heavy turtle-neck sweater, my suede coat, and my green scarf.

Taking my gloved hand in hers, she guided me through some deserted rooms toward a hall with a marble floor on which our steps resounded. Outside, in the garden with the dark trees, she helped me into the car I'd been in that afternoon.

"At ten o'clock I'm putting you to bed. I want to show you something first. In a few days, I'll let you drive."

"Would you please say the girl's name again?"

"Domenica Loi. They called her Do. When you were children, there was another girl who died a long time ago, of rheumatic fever or something of the sort. They called you cousins because you were all the same age. The other little girl was named Angela. You were all three of Italian origin: Mi, Do, and La. You see where your aunt got her nickname?"

She was driving fast, along wide, illuminated avenues.

"Your aunt's real name was Sandra Raffermi. She was your mother's sister."

"When did Mama die?"

"When you were eight or nine, I don't remember. You were put in a boarding school. Four years later your aunt got permission to take you. You'll find out sooner or later, she'd had to struggle to make ends meet in her youth. But now she was a lady, she was rich. The shoes you're wearing, the ones I'm wearing, are made in your aunt's factories."

She put her hand on my knee and said that if I liked, they were my factories, since "la Raffermi" was dead.

"Didn't you love my aunt?"

"I don't know," said Jeanne. "I love you. I don't care about the others. I was eighteen when I went to work for Raffermi. I was a heel-maker in one of her workshops

36

in Florence. I was alone, I earned my living as well as I could. That was in '42. She came one day and the first thing she gave me was a slap in the face, which I returned. She took me away with her. The last thing she gave me was also a slap, but I did not return it. That was in May of this year, a week before she died. For months she had known she was dying, which did not make her any easier to live with."

"Did I love my aunt?"

"No."

For a full minute I said nothing, trying in vain to find a face I had seen in the photographs, an old woman in a pince-nez sitting in a wheel chair.

"Did I love Domenica Loi?"

"Who could help it?" said Jeanne.

"Did I love you?"

She turned her head and I saw her face illuminated by the street lamps as they went by. She shrugged her shoulders quickly and answered in a rough voice that we were almost there. Suddenly I felt a pain as if I were being torn inside. I took her arm, and the car swerved. I apologized; undoubtedly she thought it was because of the swerve.

She showed me the Arc de Triomphe, the Place de la Concorde, the Tuileries, the Seine. After the Place Maubert, we stopped in a little street that went down to the river, before a hotel lit by a neon sign that said HOTEL VICTORIA.

We stayed in the car. She told me to look at the hotel, and saw that the building recalled nothing to me.

"What is it?" I asked.

"You've come here often. This is the hotel where Do lived."

"Let's go home, please."

She sighed, said yes, and kissed me on the temple. On the way back I pretended to fall asleep again with my head on her skirt.

She undressed me, helped me bathe, rubbed me down with a big towel, and handed me a pair of cotton gloves to replace the ones I was wearing, which were wet.

We sat down on the edge of the bathtub, she dressed, I in my nightgown. At length, it was she who took off my gloves. I looked away when I saw my hands.

She put me in the big bed, tucked me in, turned out the lamp. It was ten o'clock, as she had promised. She had had a strange expression on her face ever since she had seen the scars of the burns on my body. She had said only that they were almost gone, one spot on the back, two on the legs, and that I had lost weight. I felt that she was trying to be natural, but that she recognized me less and less.

"Don't leave me alone. I'm not used to it and I'm afraid."

She sat down beside me and stayed a moment. I fell asleep with my mouth against her hand. She did not speak. It was just before I fell asleep, in that edge of unconsciousness when everything is absurd, when everything is possible, that the idea occurred to me for the first time that I was nothing apart from what Jeanne told me about myself, and that she had only to be lying for me to be a lie.

"I want you to tell me now. For weeks I've been hear-

ing, 'later'! Yesterday you said I did not love my aunt.
Tell me why."

"Because she was not lovable."

"To me?"

"To anyone."

"If she took me in at the age of thirteen, surely she
must have loved me."

"I did not say that she didn't love you. And then, it
made her feel important. You can't understand. Loving,
not loving, you judge everything by that!"

"Why had Domenica Loi been with me since February?"

"You bumped into her in February. It was much later
that she moved in with you. Why? You're the only one
who knew that! What do you want me to say? Every
three days you had a new craze: a car, a dog, an American
poet, Domenica Loi, they were all part of the game. At
eighteen I found you in a hotel in Geneva with a little
office worker. At twenty I found you in another hotel
with Domenica Loi."

"What was she to me?"

"A slave, like everyone else."

"Like you?"

"Like me."

"What happened?"

"Nothing. What could have happened? You threw a
suitcase at me, and a vase for which I had to pay quite
a lot, and you went off with your slave."

"Where was this?"

"Residence Washington, rue Lord Byron, fourth floor,
apartment 14."

"Where did I go?"

39

"I have no idea. I wasn't interested. Your aunt was only waiting to see you before she died. When I came back I received her second slap in eighteen years. A week later, she died."

"I didn't come?"

"No. I won't say I didn't have news of you, you got into enough trouble, but not a word out of you for a month. Just about long enough for you to run out of money. And to run up so many debts that even your little gigolos lost faith in you. I got a telegram in Florence: *Forgive me, desperate, money, I kiss you a thousand times everywhere: forehead, eyes, nose, mouth, hands, feet, be nice, I'm crying, your Mi.* I assure you, that's the exact text, I'll show it to you."

She showed me the telegram when I was dressed. I read it standing with one foot on a chair while she fastened my garters, which I could not do with gloves on.

"It's a ridiculous telegram."

"And yet it's typical. There were others, you know. Sometimes it was just 'Money, Mi.' Sometimes there were fifteen telegrams in the same day all saying the same thing. You would enumerate my virtues. Or else you would line up adjectives referring to some detail of my anatomy, according to your mood. It was frightful, very expensive for an idiot who's run out of money, but at least you showed imagination."

"You talk about me as if you hated me."

"I haven't told you the words you used to use in those telegrams. You knew how to hurt. Other leg. I did not send you money after you aunt's death. I came to see you. Put your other leg on the chair. I arrived at Cap Cadet on a Sunday afternoon. You were drunk from the night before. I put you under the shower, threw out the gigolos, and emptied the ashtrays. Do helped me. You wouldn't speak to me for three days. There."

I was ready. She buttoned me into a gray serge coat, took her own coat from an adjoining room, and we left. I was living a bad dream. I no longer believed a word Jeanne was telling me.

In the car, I realized that I was still holding the telegram she had given me. Here, at least, was proof that she was not lying. We remained silent for quite a while, driving toward the Arc de Triomphe which I could see a long way ahead of us under an overcast sky.

"Where are you taking me?"

"To see Dr. Doulin. He called at the crack of dawn. He annoys me."

She glanced at me, smiling, called me her baby, and asked why I had such a long face.

"I don't want to be this Mi you're describing. I don't understand. I don't know how, but I know I'm not like that. Could I have changed that much?"

She replied that I had changed a great deal.

I spent three days reading old letters and examining the contents of the bags Jeanne had brought back from Cap Cadet.

I was trying to get to know myself systematically and Jeanne, who never left my side, sometimes had trouble making sense out of what I found: a man's shirt whose presence she could not explain; a little pearl-handled revolver, loaded, which she had never seen before; letters whose authors were unknown to her.

In spite of the gaps, I gradually formed an image of myself which did not agree with the person I had become. I was not so foolish, so vain, so violent. I had no desire to drink, to hit a stupid maid, to dance on top of a car, to fall into the arms of a Swedish racer or the first boy who came along with a pretty face. But all that might seem incomprehensible to me because of the accident, that was not what bothered me the most. Above all I could not believe myself capable of the lack of feeling that had enabled me to go out drinking the night I learned of my aunt's death and not even to come to her funeral.

"And yet it was typical," Jeanne repeated. "And then, there is nothing to indicate that it was lack of feeling. I knew you very well. You were capable of being very unhappy. This found expression in ridiculous tantrums and, more commonly for the last two years, in a pronounced need to share your bed with the whole world. Deep down, you must have felt cheated. At thirteen they have nice names for it; need for affection, the melancholy of the orphan, longing for the mother's breast. At eighteen, they use ugly medical terms."

"What did I do that was so awful?"

"It wasn't awful, it was childish."

"You never answer my questions! You let me imagine anything at all, and naturally I imagine horrible things! You do it on purpose!"

"Drink your coffee," said Jeanne.

She no longer agreed, either, with the idea I had formed of her the first afternoon and evening. She was withdrawn, more and more distant. There was something about what I said and did that she did not like, and I could see it was worrying her. She would watch me for minutes at a time without saying anything, then suddenly she would talk very fast, returning tirelessly to the story of the fire, or to that day a month before the fire when she had found me drunk at Cap Cadet.

"The best thing would be for me to go there!"

"We'll go in a few days."

"I want to see my father. Why can't I see the people I knew?"

"Your father is in Nice. He is old. It would do him no good to see you in this state. As for the others, I prefer to wait a little while."

"I don't."

"I do. Listen, sweet: it's possible that in just a few more days everything will suddenly come back to you. Do you think it's so easy for me to keep your father from seeing you? He thinks you are still in the clinic. Do you think it's so easy for me to keep off all those vultures? I want you to be cured when you see them."

Cured. I had already learned so much about myself without regaining my memory that I no longer believed in it. With Dr. Doulin there had been injections, electric shock treatments, lights in the eyes, automatic writing. They injected something into my right hand and put it behind a screen so I could not see what I was writing. I could feel neither the pencil that was placed in my hand nor the movement of my hand. While I filled three pages without being aware of it, Dr. Doulin and his assistant talked to me of the sun in the south of France, the pleasures of the seaside. This experiment, which had already been performed twice, had taught us nothing except that my handwriting had been frightfully distorted by the fact that I was wearing gloves. Dr. Doulin, whom I now trusted no more than I did Jeanne, maintained that these sessions released certain anxieties of an "unconscious personality" who did have a memory. I had read the pages I had "written." They were words without coherence, incomplete, most of them "telescoped" as in the worst days at the clinic. Those that recurred most frequently were words like nose, eyes, mouth, hands, hair, until I felt as if I were rereading Jeanne's telegram.

It was idiotic.

The "big scene" took place on the fourth day. The cook was at the other end of the house, the butler had gone out. Jeanne and I were sitting in armchairs in the living room, in front of the fireplace because I was still cold all the time. It was five o'clock in the afternoon. I had some letters and photographs in one hand and an empty cup in the other.

Jeanne was smoking. There were dark circles under her eyes, and she was again rejecting my request to see the people I had known.

"I don't wish it, that's all there is to it. Who do you think these people are? Angels from heaven? They won't let such an easy victim get away from them."

"Me, a victim? But why?"

"The reason is written in figures with a lot of zeros. You will be twenty-one in November. La Raffermi's will will be opened then, but it really isn't necessary to open it to guess the number of billion lire that will be transferred to your account."

"You should have explained all that to me too."

"I thought you knew about it."

"I know nothing, nothing! You can see very well that I know nothing!"

told from past.

She made her first blunder:

"I can't tell what you know and don't know! I'm going mad, I can't sleep any more. After all, it would be so easy for you to be putting on an act!"

She threw her cigarette into the fireplace. It was just as I was rising from my chair that the clock in the hallway struck five.

"An act? What are you talking about?"

"The amnesia!" she said. "It's a good idea, a very good idea! No brain injury, no proof, of course, but who can be sure you don't have it but you yourself?"

She had risen too, unrecognizable. Then suddenly, she was Jeanne again: light hair, golden eyes, serene face, long, slender body in a full skirt, a head taller than I.

"I don't know what I'm saying, darling."

My right hand moved before I heard her. I hit her on the side of the mouth. Pain shot up to the nape of my neck, and I fell forward onto her. She grabbed me by the shoulders, turned me around, and held me against her breast so I could not move. My arms felt so heavy that I did not try to escape.

"Calm yourself," she told me.

"Let me go! Why would I want to put on an act? For what purpose? Don't you think you should tell me that?"

"Calm yourself, please."

"I'm crazy, you've told me that often enough! But not that crazy! Why? Tell me! Let me go!"

"Will you calm down? Stop shouting!"

She made me move back, forced me to sit on her lap, in her chair. She had one arm around my shoulders and the other hand over my mouth; her head was behind mine.

"I've said nothing, or nothing of importance. Stop shouting, we'll be heard. I've been beside myself for the past three days. You have no idea!"

She made her second blunder when, her mouth next to my ear, she said in an angry whisper that frightened me more than when she raised her voice:

"You can't have made this much progress in three days without planning it! How can you walk like her, laugh like her, talk like her, if you don't remember?"

I screamed into her hand, blacked out for a second, and when I opened my eyes again I was stretched out on the carpet. Jeanne was bending over me, moistening my forehead with a handkerchief.

"Don't move, darling."

I saw the mark of the blow I had given her on one side of her face. She was bleeding a little at the corner of the mouth. So it was not a bad dream. I watched her as she unbuttoned the waistband of my skirt and lifted me again in her arms. She was afraid too.

"Drink, darling."

I swallowed something strong. I felt better. I looked at her and was calm. I said to myself that it was true that I would now be capable of putting on an act. When she drew me against her to "make up," kneeling beside me on the carpet, I mechanically put my arms around her neck. I was surprised, all at once, and almost reassured, to taste her tears on my lips.

I went to sleep very late that night. For hours I lay in bed motionless, thinking about Jeanne's words, trying to see what, from her point of view, might be my motive for simulating amnesia. I found no explanation. Nor did I guess what was bothering her, but I was certain that she had good reasons for keeping me isolated in a house where neither the cook nor the butler knew who I was. What these were I might well know by tomorrow: since she still would not let me see the people I had known, I had only to call on one of them to bring about precisely what she wanted to avoid. I would see for myself.

What I had to do was look up one of my friends who was living in Paris. The one I chose—I had his address on the back of an envelope—was the boy who had written me that I would belong to him always.

His name was Francois Chance, he lived on the Boulevard Suchet. Jeanne had told me that he was a lawyer, and that he had not had much of a "chance" with the old Mi.

While waiting to fall asleep, I lived twenty times over the plan I had devised for escaping Jeanne's supervision the next day. This state of mind seemed about to recall another moment of my life, but it passed. Sleep overtook me as for the twentieth time I was getting out of a white Fiat 1500 in a Paris street.

I slammed the car door.

"Where are you going? Wait for me!"

She got out of the car too and caught up with me on the sidewalk. I shrugged off her arm.

"I'll be all right. I just want to walk around a little and look at the windows, be by myself! Don't you understand that I need to be alone?"

I showed her the folder I had in my hand. Some newspaper clippings fell out of it and scattered on the pavement. She helped me collect them. They were the articles that had appeared after the fire. Dr. Doulin had given them to me after a session of lights and inkblot tests:

wasted effort, a lost hour which I would have preferred to use admitting my real anxieties. Unfortunately Jeanne insisted on being present at our interviews.

She took me by the shoulders, tall, elegant, hair golden in the midday sun. I pulled away again.

"You're not being sensible, darling," she told me. "It's almost time for lunch. This afternoon I'll take you for a ride in the park."

"No. Please, Jeanne. I need this."

"Very well, then, I'll follow you."

She left me and got back into her car. She was annoyed but not furious, as I had expected. I walked along the sidewalk about a hundred yards, ran into a group of girls coming out of their office or factory, and crossed the street. I stopped in front of a lingerie shop. When I turned my eyes I saw the Fiat pull up opposite me, double-parked. I walked back to Jeanne. She leaned across the empty seat and rolled down the window.

"Give me some money," I said.

"What for?"

"I want to buy some things."

"In that store? I can take you to better shops than that."

"That's where I want to go. Give me some money, plenty. I want a lot of things."

She raised her eyebrows in resignation. I waited for her to accuse me of acting like a twelve-year-old, but she said nothing. She opened her purse, took out the bills that were in it, and gave them to me.

"Don't you want me to come and help you decide? I'm the only one who knows what you can wear."

"I'll be fine."

As I was going into the shop, I heard behind me,

"Size 12, dear!" To the saleswoman who came to greet me at the door I pointed out a dress on a mannequin, some slips and underwear, a sweater in the window.

I said that I did not have time to try anything on and that I wanted separate packages. Then I opened the door again and called Jeanne. She got out of the car, her face stamped with fatigue.

"It's too expensive. Would you write me a check?"

She went into the store ahead of me. While she was making out the check I took the first packages that were ready, said I was taking them to the car, and left.

On the dashboard of the Fiat I left the note I had in the pocket of my coat: "Jeanne, don't worry, don't try to find me, I'll meet you at the house or else call. You have nothing to fear from me. I don't know what you're afraid of, but I kiss the place where I hit you, because I love you and I feel badly about it: I have started to resemble your lies."

As I was walking away a policeman came and told me that the car could not stay double-parked. I replied that as it was not mine, I had nothing to do with it.

I WOULD HAVE MURDERED

THE TAXI TOOK ME to the Boulevard Suchet and left me in front of a new-looking building with large bay windows. I saw the name of the man I was looking for on a plate in the hallway. I climbed three flights of stairs, out of some nameless fear of the elevator, and rang the doorbell without thinking twice. Friend, lover, admirer, vulture, what difference did it make?

The door was opened by a man of thirty, tall, good-looking, in a gray suit. I heard people talking in the apartment.

"Francois Chance?"

"He's out for lunch. You wanted to see him? He didn't tell me he had an appointment."

"I don't have an appointment."

Undecided, he showed me into a large vestibule with bare walls and no furniture, leaving the door open. I did not feel as if I had met him before, but he looked me up and down in a strange manner. I asked him who he was.

"Who am I? Who are you?"

"I am Michele Isola. I just got out of the clinic. I know Francois. I wanted to talk to him."

It was obvious from his bewildered expression that this man also knew Michele Isola. He walked away slowly, shaking his head twice as if in doubt, then said, "Excuse me," and dashed into a room at the end of the vestibule. He returned with a man who was older, heavier, less attractive, who was still holding a napkin in his hand and had not swallowed his last mouthful.

"Micky!"

He was fifty, perhaps, with a receding hairline and a soft face. He threw his napkin to the man who had answered the door and came toward me with huge strides.

"Come, we can't stay here. Why didn't you call? Come."

He took me into a room and closed the door. He put his hands on my shoulders and held me before him at arm's length. I had to undergo this scrutiny for several seconds.

"Well, if this isn't a surprise! Of course I would hardly have known you, but you're lovely and you seem fine. Sit down. Tell me about yourself. Your memory?"

"You know about that?"

"Of course I know about it! Murneau called me again day before yesterday. Didn't she come with you?"

The room must have been his office. There was a big mahogany table covered with files, plain armchairs, glass-covered bookcases.

"When did you leave the clinic? This morning? You haven't done anything foolish, have you?"

"Who are you?"

He sat down facing me and took my gloved hand. The question disconcerted him, but from the expression on his face—surprised, amused, then distressed—I could watch it travel rapidly through his mind.

"You don't know who I am and yet you come to see me? What's going on? Where's Murneau?"

"She doesn't know I'm here."

I sensed that he was having a series of surprises, that things must be simpler than I thought. He dropped my hand.

"If you don't remember me, how do you know my address?"

"From your letter."

"What letter?"

"The one I got at the clinic."

"I didn't write to you."

It was my turn to look surprised. He was looking at me the way one looks at an animal. I saw from his expression that it was not my memory he doubted, but my sanity.

"Just a moment," he said suddenly. "Don't move."

I rose as he did and blocked his way to the telephone. In spite of myself I raised my voice and began shouting.

"Don't do that! I did get a letter, your address was on the envelope. I came to find out who you were, and for you to tell me who I am!"

"Calm yourself. I don't understand a word you're

saying. If Murneau doesn't know about this, I must call her. I don't know how you got out of that clinic, but obviously it was without anyone's permission."

He took me by the shoulders again and tried to make me sit down in the chair I had left. He was very pale at the temples but his cheeks had suddenly flushed.

"I beg of you, you must explain to me! I've had some strange ideas, but I'm not crazy. Please!"

He gave up trying to make me sit down. I took him by the arm as he made another dive for the phone on the table.

"Calm yourself," he said. "I wish you no harm. I've known you for years."

"Who are you?"

"Francois! I'm a lawyer. I handle Raffermi's business. I'm on 'The Register.' "

" 'The Register'?"

"The account book, the people who worked for her, who were on her payroll. I'm a friend, it would take too long to explain. I was the one who handled your contracts in France, see? Sit down."

"You didn't write me after the accident?"

"No. Murneau asked me not to. I asked after you as everyone did, but I did not write. What am I supposed to have said?"

"That I would belong to you always."

As I repeated the words, I realized how absurd it was to imagine this man with the heavy face who could have been my father writing a letter like that.

"What? That's ridiculous! I'd never take such a liberty! Where is this letter?"

"I don't have it with me."

"Listen, Micky, I don't know what's in your head. It's

possible that in the state you're in, you imagine all sorts of things. But please let me call Murneau."

"Actually it was Jeanne who gave me the idea of coming to see you. I got a love letter from you, then Jeanne told me that you 'never had a chance' with me: what was I to think?"

"Did Murneau read this letter?"

"I have no idea."

"I don't understand," he said. "If Murneau told you that I never had a 'chance' with you, first of all it's because you used to make that play on words, and then because she was talking about something else. It's true you caused me a lot of trouble."

"Trouble?"

"Let's not talk about it, please. A matter of childish debts, dented fenders, it's not important. Sit down, that's a good girl, and let me call. Have you had any lunch?"

I did not dare stop him again. I let him walk around his table and dial the number. I backed slowly toward the door. As he listened to the phone ringing at the other end of the wire he did not take his eyes off me, but it was obvious that he did not see me.

"Do you know if she's at your place right now?"

He hung up and dialed again. At my place? So she had not told him, any more than she had the others, where she was keeping me, since he thought I had left the clinic this morning. I realized that before coming to get me, she must have lived somewhere else for several weeks, somewhere that was "my place," and it was there that he was calling

"There's no answer."

"Where are you calling?"

"Rue de Courcelles, of course. Is she out for lunch?"

I heard him call "Micky!" behind me but I was already in the vestibule, opening the front door. My legs had never felt so tired, but the steps were wide, Aunt Midola's shoes were well made, and I did not fall down the stairs.

For a quarter of an hour I walked through empty streets near the Porte d'Auteuil. I realized that I still had Dr. Doulin's folder of newspaper clippings under my arm. I stopped in front of a mirror in a shop window to make sure my beret was on right, that I did not look like a criminal. I saw a girl with drawn features, but calm and well dressed, and behind her I saw the man who had answered the door at Francois Chance's apartment.

Instinctively I clapped my free hand over my mouth and jerked around with a start that hurt from the shoulders to the crown of my head.

"Don't be afraid, Micky, I'm a friend. Come, I must talk to you."

"Who are you?"

"Don't be afraid, please come. I just want to talk to you."

He took my arm gently. I relaxed: we were too far away for him to force me to go back to Francois Chance's.

"You followed me?"

"Yes. When you came just now I lost my head. I didn't recognize you, you didn't seem to know me. I waited for you outside the building in my car, but you left in such a hurry I couldn't stop you. Then you turned into a one-way street, and I had a hard time finding you."

He held onto me firmly until we reached his car, a black sedan parked in a square I had just crossed.

"Where are you taking me?"

"Wherever you like. You haven't had lunch? Do you remember the Chez Reine?"

"No."

"It's a restaurant. We used to go there often, you and I. Micky, I assure you you have no reason to be afraid."

He squeezed my arm and said very quickly, "It was me you came to see this morning. I was beginning to think you'd never come back. I didn't know about . . . well, that you couldn't remember who you were. I didn't know what to think any more."

He had very dark, bright eyes and a rather monotonous but pleasant voice that went well with his high-strung personality. He seemed strong and troubled. For some reason I did not like him, but I was not afraid of him any more.

"Did you listen at the door?"

"I heard from the hall. Get in, please. The letter was from me. My name is Francois too, Francois Roussin. You made a mistake because of the address. . . ."

When I was sitting next to him in the car he asked me to use the familiar you with him, as I had before. I was incapable of coherent thought. I watched him get out his key, put it in the ignition; I was amazed to see his hand tremble. I was even more amazed that I was not trembling myself. I must have loved this man, since he was my lover. It was natural for him to be nervous on seeing me again. I felt numb all over. If I shivered, it was because I was cold. Nothing was real but the cold.

I had kept my coat on. I had the feeling that the wine was warming me. I was drinking much too much and my mind was not any clearer for it.

56

I had met him the year before at Francois Chance's, where he worked. I had spent ten days in Paris in the fall. His story of how our affair began implied that it was not my first. I had actually spirited him away from his work and shut him up with me in a hotel in Milly la Forêt. When I returned to Florence I had written him passionate letters which he would show me. Of course I was unfaithful to him, but it was out of bravado, out of boredom because I missed him. I tried unsuccessfully to arrange a trumped-up business trip to Italy with my aunt. We got together again in January of this year when I came to Paris. *Grande passion.*

The end of the affair, for there must inevitably have been one (the accident), seemed to me as vague as possible. Perhaps it was partly the effect of the wine, but events became more and more confused after the arrival of Domenica Loi on the scene.

There had been a quarrel, broken dates, another quarrel in which I had slapped him, another quarrel in which I had not slapped but beaten up Do, so violently that she went down on her knees to me and bore the bruises for a week. There had also been an episode apparently unconnected with the main action in which there was some question of dishonesty on the part of someone— him, me, or Do. And then, things no longer connected with anything: jealousy, a nightclub on the Étoile, the mysterious influence of a diabolical character (Do) who was trying to keep me away from him (Francois), a sudden departure in an MG in the month of June, unanswered letters, the return of the Monster (Jeanne), the more and more mysterious influence of the diabolical character over the Monster, a worried voice on the telephone (mine) during a long distance call from Paris to Cap Cadet which had lasted twenty-five minutes and cost him a fortune.

Since he talked continuously, he did not eat. He ordered a second bottle of wine, was very restless and smoked a great deal. He guessed that everything he was telling me sounded untrue. After a while he was repeating "I assure you" at the end of every sentence. I had a lump of ice in my chest. When all at once I thought of Jeanne, I felt like putting my head on my arms on the tablecloth and going to sleep, or sobbing. She would find me, she would put my beret back on my head, she would take me away from all this, away from this ugly, monotonous voice, this noise of crockery, this smoke which was irritating my eyes.

"Let's leave."

"Give me a second, please. Don't go away! I have to call the office."

If I had not been so numb and depressed, I would have left. I lit a cigarette which I could not bear and immediately put out in my plate. I said to myself that if it had been told differently, this story would not have seemed so ugly to me, I might have recognized myself in it. From the outside nothing is true. But who could know, if I did not, what that little scatterbrain had in her heart? When I recovered my memory, the events would probably be the same, but the story behind them would be different.

"Come on," he said. "You're worn out. You can't go like this."

He took my arm again. He opened a glass door. There was sunlight on the quays. I was sitting in his car. We were driving through sloping streets.

"Where are we going?"

"To my place. Listen, Micky, I know I've told all this very badly, I wish you'd forget it. We'll talk about it again when you've slept a little. All these shocks, all these constant emotions, I understand you're upset. Don't be too quick to misjudge me."

He put his hand on my knee as he drove, as Jeanne had done.

"It's wonderful to see you again," he said.

When I awoke, night had just fallen. I had the worst headache I had had since the first days at the clinic. Francois shook my arm.

"I've made you some coffee. I'll get it for you."

I was in a room with drawn shades and odd furniture. The bed on which I was lying in my sweater and skirt, a blanket over my legs, was a folding sofa-bed, and I remembered Francois fixing it. On a little table on a level with my eyes I saw a photograph of myself, at least the person I was "before," in a silver frame. At the foot of an armchair facing the bed, Dr. Doulin's newspaper clippings were spread out on the rug. Francois must have read them while I was asleep.

He returned with a steaming cup. It made me feel better. He smiled as he watched me drink, his hands in the pockets of his trousers; he was in shirt sleeves, apparently very pleased with himself. I looked at my watch; it had stopped.

"Have I been asleep long?"

"It's six o'clock. Feeling better?"

"I feel as if I could still sleep for ages. I have a head-ache."

"Is there something we should do?" he asked.

"I don't know."

"Do you want me to call a doctor?"

He sat down on the bed next to me, and took the empty cup I was holding. He put it on the rug.

"It would be better if you called Jeanne."

"There's a doctor in the building, but I don't have the telephone number. And then I'll admit I have no desire to see her here again."

"Don't you like her?"

He laughed and took me in his arms. "I've found you again," he said. "You haven't really changed. There are those we love and those we don't love. No, don't go away. I have a right to hold you a little after all this time."

He made me lower my head, ran his hand through my hair, and kissed me gently on the back of my neck.

"No, I don't like her. You, you have to love the whole world. Even that poor girl who still, God knows . . ."

Still holding me in his arms, he waved his hand to indicate the newspaper clippings on the rug.

"I read those. I had already heard the story, but all those details—it's horrible. I'm glad you tried to get her out of there. Let me see your hair."

Quickly I put my hand on my head. "No, please."

"Do you have to keep these gloves on?" he asked.

"Please."

He kissed my gloved hand, lifted it gently, stroked my hair.

"That's what changes you the most, your hair. At lunch before, a couple of times I felt as if I were talking to a stranger."

He took my face in his hands and looked at me for a long time closely. "And yet, it's really you, it's really

Micky. I watched you sleep. I've often watched you sleep, you know. Just now, your face was the same."

He kissed me on the mouth: a chaste little kiss at first, to see how I would react, then a longer one. Another languor overtook me which was nothing like the one at lunch: a sweet pain all through my body. A sensation which came from before the clinic, before the white light, simply from "before." I did not move. I was alert, and I think I had the absurd hope of recovering everything in one kiss. I pulled away because I could no longer breathe.

"Do you believe me now?" he asked.

He had a smug little smile on his face, one brown lock on his forehead. It was that remark that spoiled everything. I pulled farther away.

"Did I come to this room often?"

"Not very often, no. I used to come to see you."

"Where?"

"At La Residence, rue Lord Byron, and then rue de Courcelles. Look, here's proof!"

Suddenly he got up, went and opened some drawers, and returned with a small bunch of keys.

"You gave them to me when you moved into rue de Courcelles. There were nights when you did not have dinner with me, and we would meet there."

"An apartment?"

"No, a small private hotel. Very nice. Murneau will show you. Or if you like, we'll go together. We were happy there."

"Tell me about it."

He laughed again, putting his arms around me. I lay back on the bed, the keys hard in the palm of my hand.

"About what?" he asked.

"Us. Jeanne. Do."

"Us, that's interesting. But not La Murneau, or the other one. It was because of the other one that I stopped coming."

"Why?"

"She turned you against me. After you took her down there, nothing went right any more. You were crazy. You had crazy ideas."

"When was that?"

"I've forgotten. Just before you left for the south, the two of you."

"What was she like?"

"Look, she's dead. I don't like to speak ill of the dead. And then, what does it matter what she was like? You saw her differently: a nice girl, a darling, who would have done anything for you. And so intelligent! Yes, she must have been intelligent. She knew just how to manipulate you and Murneau. To tell the truth she came within an inch of manipulating old lady Raffermi too."

"Had she met my aunt?"

"No, fortunately. But if your aunt had died a month later, you can be sure she would have met her, she would have had her slice of the cake. You were planning to take her there. She was so eager to see Italy!"

"Why do you think she turned me against you?"

"I was in her way."

"Why?"

"As if I knew! She thought you were going to marry me. You were wrong to tell her about our plans. And we're wrong to talk about all this now. Let's stop."

He kissed me on the neck, on the mouth, but I no

longer felt anything, I was immobile, trying to organize my thoughts.

"Why did you say a little while ago that you were glad I tried to get her out of the room during the fire?"

"Because if it had been me, I would have said the hell with it. And then, other things. Let's stop, Micky."

"What things? I want to know."

"When I heard about this I was in Paris. I didn't understand very well what had happened. God knows what I imagined. I didn't believe it was an accident. At least, not a real accident."

I was speechless. He was mad. He was saying horrible things while slowly lifting my skirt with one hand and unbuttoning the neck of my sweater with the other. I tried to sit up.

"Leave me alone."

"Stop thinking about all that, do you understand!"

He pushed me roughly back onto the bed. I tried to push away the hand that was climbing up my legs again, but it was he who pushed mine away, hurting me.

"Leave me alone!"

"Listen, Micky! . . ."

"Why did you think it was not an accident?"

"Good God! You'd have to be nuts to believe it was an accident, knowing Murneau! You'd have to be nuts to believe she would have overlooked a bad connection for the three weeks she stayed down there! You can be dead sure that connection was perfectly all right!"

I struggled as well as I could. He would not release me, the struggle aroused him to fight harder. He tore the neck of my sweater and this was what stopped him. He saw that I was crying and let me go.

I looked for my coat and shoes. I did not hear what he was saying. I collected the newspaper clippings and put them back in the folder. I noticed that I still had the keys he had given me in one hand. I put them in the pocket of my coat.

He stood in front of the door to block my way, a strangely submissive look on his tired face. I wiped my eyes with the back of my hand and told him that if he wanted to see me again, he would have to let me go.

"This is crazy, Micky. It's crazy, I tell you. I've been thinking about you for months. I don't know what came over me."

He stood on the landing watching me go down the stairs. Sad, ugly, greedy, false: a vulture.

I walked for a long time. I turned into one street after another. The more I thought, the more confused my ideas became. The pain beginning in the back of my neck radiated into my back and all along my spine. It was probably because of my fatigue that it happened.

I had been walking first to find a taxi, then just to walk, because I no longer wanted to go back to Neuilly, to see Jeanne. I thought of calling her, but I would not have been able to keep from mentioning the connection. I was afraid that if she justified herself I would not believe her.

I was cold. I went into a café to get warm. As I was paying, I noticed that she had given me a great deal of money, undoubtedly enough to live on for several days. To live, at that moment, meant only one thing: to be able to lie down, to be able to sleep. I would also have liked to wash, change my clothes, change my gloves.

I walked some more and went into a hotel near the

Gare Montparnasse. They asked me whether I had any baggage, whether I wanted a room with a bath, they made me fill out a form. I paid in advance.

As I was following a maid up the stairs, the manager called me from the desk:

"Mademoiselle Loi, do you need to be called in the morning?"

I answered no, it would not be necessary, then I turned around, cold all over, my mind congealed with fear, because I had already known, I had known for a long time, I had always known.

"What did you call me?"

He looked at the form I had filled out.

"Mademoiselle Loi. Isn't that right?"

I walked down to him. I was still trying to suppress an old fear. It couldn't be true, it was simply a case of "telescoping," the fact that I had talked about her two hours before, fatigue. . . .

I had written on this yellow paper: *Loi, Domenica Lella Marie, born July 4, 1939 in Nice (Alpes-Maritimes), French, bank employee.*

The signature was *Doloi,* written very legibly as one word and surrounded by an awkward and hurried oval.

I undressed. I ran a bath. I took off my gloves before slipping into the water. Then, since I could not bear to touch my body with my hands, I put them on again.

I moved slowly, almost calmly. At a certain degree of prostration, to be dead tired and to be calm amounted to the same thing.

I no longer knew in what direction to think so I did not think at all. I felt ill and at the same time I felt good because the water was warm. I remained this way

65

for perhaps an hour. I had not reset my watch and when I looked at it, as I got out of the bathtub, it still pointed to three o'clock in the afternoon.

I dried myself with the hotel towels, put on my underwear with burning hands and wet gloves. The mirror on the wardrobe reflected the image of an automaton with narrow hips, walking barefoot around the room with a face that was less human than ever. Coming closer, I noticed that the bath had brought out hideous lines on the eyebrows, the wings of the nose, the chin, the ears. Underneath the hair the scars were swollen, brick red.

I fell on the bed and lay a long time with my head in my arms with only one thought: a girl deliberately plunging her hands and face into the fire.

It was not possible. Who could have that kind of courage? I suddenly became aware of the presence a few inches from my eye of the file Dr. Doulin had turned over to me.

The first time I had glanced through the articles this morning, everything had agreed with Jeanne's account. On rereading them I discovered some details which had seemed unimportant at the time but which now stared me in the face.

Neither Domenica Loi's date of birth nor her other given names had been mentioned. It said only that she was twenty-one years old. But since the fire had occurred on July 4, they added that the unfortunate girl had died on the night of her birthday. I thought for a few seconds that I could have known Do's names and the date of her birth just as well as she, I could have written Loi instead of Isola: my fatigue, the preoccupations of which she was a part, everything explained it.

But this did not explain such a total split: the whole form, down to that silly schoolgirl's signature.

Other objections crowded into my mind. Jeanne could not be mistaken. She had helped me bathe from the first evening, for years she had been a second mother to me. If my face had changed, my body, my walk, my voice had not. Do might have been the same height as I, might even have had the same color eyes and hair, but the mistake was not possible for Jeanne. The curve of a back or shoulder, the shape of a leg would have betrayed me.

I said the word to myself: betrayed. And it was bizarre, as if already, in spite of myself, my mind had traveled toward an explanation which I did not want to admit, any more than I had wanted to admit for several days now the obvious signs of what I had discovered when I reread the hotel register.

I was not myself! Even my inability to recover my past was a proof. How could I have recovered the past of someone I was not?

Furthermore, Jeanne had not recognized me. My laugh surprised her, my walk, other details I did not know, which she perhaps attributed to convalescence, but which were preying on her mind and gradually estranging her from me.

This was what I had set out to learn today when I ran away from her. Her "I can't sleep any more," her "How can you look like her?" I looked like Do, for God's sake! Jeanne did not want to admit it any more than I did, but every gesture I made weighed on her heart, every night of doubt put new circles under her eyes.

There was, however, a flaw in this reasoning: the night of the fire. Jeanne was there. She had picked me up at the foot of the stairs, she had certainly accompanied me to La Ciotat, to Nice. She had also been asked to identify the body of the dead girl before her parents were. Even burned, I was recognizable. The mistake was possible for a stranger, but not for Jeanne.

So it was just the opposite: simpler, but more horrible. "Who's to tell me you're not putting on an act?" Jeanne was afraid, afraid of me. Not because I was looking more and more like Do, *but because she knew I was Do!*

She had known it since the night of the fire. Why she had kept quiet, why she had lied, I hated to imagine. It was horrible to think of Jeanne deliberately taking the living girl for the dead one in order to keep her little heiress alive, in spite of everything, until the reading of a will.

She had kept quiet, but there was still one witness to her lie: the living girl. This was what kept her awake at night. She had isolated the witness, who was perhaps putting on an act, perhaps not, and she had to keep on lying. She was no longer completely sure of her mistake, of her own memory, she was no longer sure of anything. How was she to recognize a smile, the location of a mole after three months' absence and three days' new habits? She had everything to fear: first, from those who had known the dead girl well and who might uncover fraud; above all, from me, whom she was keeping away from the others. She did not know how I would react when I recovered my memory.

There was another flaw, however: on the night of the fire, Jeanne could have found a girl without face or hands, but she could not have suspected that she would be a perfect automaton whose past was as blank as her future. It was hard to believe that she would have taken such risks. Unless . . .

Unless the witness had as much reason as she for keeping quiet, and—why not, since I had embarked on these vile and impossible suppositions—that realizing this, Jeanne was convinced that she herself would have a hold over me. This was where Francois' suspicions regarding the connection came in. It seemed to me, as it had to him, that a defect of installation flagrant enough to cause a fire could not have escaped her notice. Therefore the connection must have been in order. Therefore, someone must have tampered with it afterward.

If the investigators and insurance people had maintained the hypothesis of an accident, the damage could not have been done all at once, simply by cutting a wire. In several of the articles I found details: a coupling which had been corroded by dampness for several weeks, the sides of a water pipe which had been rusted. This implied preparation, a slow process. There was a name for this: murder.

It was before the fire that the girl who was alive had chosen to take the place of the dead one! Since Mi had no interest in this substitution, the one who was alive was Do. I was alive: I was Do. From a hotel register to the pipe of a water heater, the circle was complete, just like that pretentious oval surrounding the signature.

I found myself, how nor for how long I did not know, kneeling under the washbowl in my hotel room examining the pipes, getting dust on my gloves. They were not gas pipes, they must be very different from the ones at Cap Cadet, but I must have had some vague hope that they would prove the absurdity of my hypotheses. I said to myself, it's not true, you're going too fast, even if the connection was well made, something could have gone wrong naturally. I answered myself, the installation was barely three months old, it's impossible, and anyway no one believed it was possible, since they came to the conclusion that there was an initial defect.

I was in my slip: I was very cold again. I put on my skirt and my torn sweater. I had to give up trying to put my stockings on. I rolled them into a ball which I put in my coat pocket. Such was my state of mind that even in this act I found a proof: Mi certainly would not have done it. A pair of stockings was not that important to her. She would have thrown them anywhere, across the room.

In the pocket of the coat I felt the keys Francois had given me. This, I think, was the third nice thing life did for me that day. The second was a kiss, until a voice said, "Do you believe me now?" The first was the look on Jeanne's face when I had asked her to make out a check and she had got out of the car. It was a weary look, slightly annoyed, but in it I had read that she loved me with all her heart: and I had only to think of it, in this hotel room, to believe again that none of what I was imagining was true.

In the phone book the private hotel on the rue de Courcelles was in the name of Raffermi. My index finger in its damp cotton glove passed fifty-four numbers in the column before it stopped at the right one.

The taxi left me in front of number fifty-five: a doorway with a high, black, wrought-iron gate. My watch, which I had reset when I left the hotel in Montparnasse, pointed to almost midnight.

Beyond a garden planted with chestnut trees, the house stood white, tall, and peaceful. There was no light and the shutters looked closed.

I opened the gate, which did not creak, and walked up a path bordered with grass. My keys did not fit the locks on the front door. I went around the house and found a service door, which I opened.

Inside there were still traces of Jeanne's perfume. I turned the lights on in the rooms as I came to them. They were small, mostly painted white, and furnished in a style I found warm and comfortable. On the second floor I found the bedrooms. They opened onto a hallway which was half white, half nothing, probably because they had not finished painting the walls.

The first room I went into was Micky's bedroom. I did not ask myself how I knew it was hers. Everything spoke of her: the disorder of the pictures on one wall, the richness of the fabrics, the big canopy bed ringed with muslin which the draft from the hallway swelled when I entered like the sails of a ship. Then too, the tennis rackets on the table, the photograph of a boy pinned to a lampshade, the big plush elephant sitting in an armchair, the German officer's cap on a stone bust that must have been Godmother Midola.

I opened the curtains of the bed to lie down for a few seconds, then the drawers of the furniture to see if, contrary to all expectation, I could find some proof that this room belonged to me. I took out underwear, objects which meant nothing to me, some papers which I glanced through quickly and dropped onto the rug.

I left the room in great disorder, but what difference did it make? I knew I was going to call Jeanne. I would put my past, my present, and my future in her hands, I would go to sleep. She would take care of disorder and murder alike.

The second room was anonymous, the third was the one Jeanne must have slept in while I was at the clinic. The perfume lingering in the adjoining bathroom, the size of the garments in the wardrobe told me this.

At last I opened the door of the room I was looking for. There was nothing left but the furniture, a little underwear in a chest of drawers, a green and blue plaid bathrobe with "Do" embroidered on the upper pocket, and three suitcases near the bed.

The suitcases were full. I realized, as I dumped their contents onto the rug, that Jeanne had brought them from Cap Cadet. Two of them contained things of Mi's which she had not shown me. If they were in this room, perhaps it was because Jeanne did not have the courage to go into the dead girl's room. Or perhaps for no reason.

The third bag, which was smaller, contained very little clothing, but some letters and papers belonging to Do. There was too little for me to think that this was all, but I told myself that the Lois had probably been given the rest of their daughter's belongings that had escaped the fire.

I untied a piece of string holding several letters together. They were letters from Godmother Midola (as she signed herself) to someone I at first thought was Mi, because they began "My dear," or "*Carina,*" or "My little girl." As I read them, I realized that since they frequently referred to Mi, they must be addressed to Do. Perhaps I had a strange idea of spelling now, but they seemed to me to be crawling with mistakes. They were very tender, however, and what I read there, between the lines, chilled my blood again.

Before continuing my inventory, I looked for a telephone. There was one in Mi's room. I called the Neuilly number. It was almost one o'clock in the morning, but Jeanne must have had her hand on the receiver, for she picked it up immediately. Before I could say a word, she expressed her anxiety, half scolding, half pleading with me. I begged her to stop.

"Where are you?"

"Rue de Courcelles."

There was a sudden, prolonged silence, which could have meant anything: astonishment, or confession. It was I who finally broke it: "Come, I'm waiting for you."

"How are you?"

"Not well. Bring me some gloves."

I hung up. I went back to Do's room and continued going through *my* papers. Then I took a pair of panties and a slip that had belonged to me, and the plaid bathrobe. I changed my clothes. I even took off my shoes. Barefoot, I went down to the ground floor. The only thing left that belonged to the "other" was my gloves, and those were mine.

In the living room I turned on all the lights and took a swallow of cognac out of the bottle. I spent a long time figuring out the mechanism of a record player. I put on something loud. The cognac made me feel better, but I did not dare drink more of it. I took the bottle anyway and went and lay down in an adjacent room that seemed warmer, and I held it against my breast in the darkness.

About twenty minutes after my telephone call, I heard a door open. A moment later the music stopped in the next room. Steps came toward the room where I was. Jeanne did not turn on the light. I saw her long silhouette pause on the threshold with one hand on the doorknob—exactly like the negative of the young woman who had appeared to me at the clinic. She remained silent for several seconds and then in her sweet, low, calm voice she said, "Good evening, Do."

I SHALL MURDER

IT ALL BEGAN one February afternoon at the bank where Do worked, through what Mi later called (and of course one was expected to laugh) *"un coup de chance."* * The check looked like every other one that passed through Domenica's hands between nine in the morning and five at night without any interruption other than the forty-five minutes for lunch. It carried the signature of the holder of the account, Francois Chance, and it was only after carrying out the withdrawal procedure that Domenica read the endorsement: MICHELE ISOLA.

Almost mechanically, she looked over the heads of her colleagues and saw on the other side of the tellers' coun-

* "A stroke of luck," a pun on the name of the lawyer who signed Mi's checks. ——*Translator.*

ter a girl with blue eyes, long black hair, and a beige coat. She remained seated, more amazed by Mi's beauty than by her presence. God knew how often she had imagined this meeting: once it had taken place on an ocean liner (an ocean liner!), another time at the theater (where she never went), or else on an Italian beach (she had never been to Italy): in short, anywhere at all in a world that was not really real, where she was not really Do, the world of "just before sleep," when you are free to imagine anything at all.

Behind a counter which she had been seeing every day for two years, fifteen minutes before the closing bell, the meeting was even less real, but it did not surprise her. And yet Mi was so pretty, so dazzling, she seemed so wonderfully in tune with life, that the sight of her swept away all the dreams.

Home in bed, life was simpler. There Do found an orphan whom she surpassed in height (five feet six inches), learning (graduated with high honors), judgment (she multiplied Mi's fortune by means of nebulous financial transactions), courage (she saved Godmother Midola from a shipwreck while Mi thought only of herself and perished), success (Mi's future fiancé, an Italian prince, preferred the poor "cousin" three days before the wedding: dreadful pangs of conscience)—in short, in everything. As for beauty, that went without saying.

Mi was so lovely that over fifteen feet away, over the heads of people coming and going, it made Do almost sick to her stomach. She wanted to get up but she could not. She saw the check disappear into a pile of others, the pile pass into the hands of one of her colleagues, then on to one of the tellers. The girl in the beige coat

—from a distance she seemed over twenty and very sure of herself—put the money that was handed to her into her bag, flashed a smile, and walked to the door of the bank, where another girl was waiting for her.

Domenica walked around the counters with a curious sensation of nausea in her chest. She said to herself, "I'm going to lose her, I'll never see her again. If I see her, if I have the nerve to talk to her, she'll honor me with a smile and forget me a minute later."

This was almost what happened. She caught up with the two girls on the Boulevard Saint Michel, more than fifty yards from the bank, as they were about to get into a white MG which was illegally parked. Mi looked politely but without recognition at this girl in a blouse who was taking her by the sleeve, who must be dying of cold (she was), who had been running and was speaking in a breathless voice.

Do said that she was Do. After much explanation, Mi seemed to recall her little childhood companion and said that it was funny to meet like this. Already, there was nothing else to say. It was Mi who made the effort. She asked how long Do had been living in Paris and working in a bank, how she liked her job. She introduced Do to her friend, a messy American girl who was already in the car. Then she said, "Call me one of these days. It was fun seeing you again."

They left, Mi at the wheel, with the roar of a motor gunned to the limit. Do got back to the bank just as the doors were closing, her mind full of confusion and bitterness. *How can I call her, I don't even know where she lives. It's amazing she's as tall as I am, she used to be much shorter. I'd be as pretty as she is if I were dressed like that. How much was that check for? A lot she cares whether I call her or not. She doesn't have an Italian accent. What a fool I am, she was the one who had to make conversation. She must have thought me stupid and a mess. I hate her. Well, I can hate her as much as I please, I'm the one who'll choke on it.*

She stayed and worked for an hour after closing. She found the check just as the other employees were getting ready to leave. Mi's address was not on it. She made a note of the address of the account holder, Francois Chance.

She called him half an hour later, from the Dupont-Latin. She said she was Mi's cousin, that she had just run into her, that she had forgotten to ask her telephone number. The man on the other end of the wire said that to his knowledge Mlle. Isola had no cousin, but finally he gave her the number and an address: Residence Washintgon, rue Lord Byron.

As she was leaving the phone booth in the basement, Do gave herself three full days before calling Mi. Upstairs she met some people who were waiting for her: two friends from work, and a boy she had known for six months, been kissing for four and sleeping with for two. He was thin, nice, a bit of a dreamer, not bad looking, an insurance broker.

Do sat down beside him, looked at him, found him less nice, less attractive, less of a dreamer, and just as much of an insurance broker. She went down to the basement again and called Mi, who was out.

She got the girl without an Italian accent on the phone five days later, after trying several times every night between six and twelve. On the evening in question, she was calling from the apartment of Gabriel, the insurance broker, who was sleeping beside her with his head under the pillow. It was midnight.

Against all reasonable doubt, Mi remembered the meeting. She apologized for having been out. It was hard to catch her in the evenings—or the mornings, for that matter.

Do, who had prepared all sorts of clever ways of getting to see her, could only say, "I must talk to you."

"Okay," said Mi. "Come on over, but make it soon, I'm tired. I love you, but I have to get up early tomorrow."

She made a kissing noise with her mouth and hung up. Do sat on the edge of the bed for several minutes with the receiver in her hand, like an idiot. Then she leaped for her clothes.

"You're leaving?" asked Gabriel.

Half-dressed, she hugged him, laughing hysterically. Gabriel thought she was completely mad and put his pillow back over his head. He had to get up early too.

It was big, luxurious, very English: a kind of hotel, with a uniformed doorman, and men in black behind dark counters. They called Mi on the telephone to announce the arrival.

Do saw a bar at the end of the lobby which you entered by walking down three steps. In it people were sitting, people who must be the kind you meet on ocean liners, on fashionable beaches, at theater *premières:* the world of "just before sleep."

The man stopped the elevator at the fourth floor. Apartment 14: Do checked her appearance in a hall mirror, patted her hair, which she had arranged in a heavy bun because it took too much time to do it loose.

The bun made her seem a little older and gave her a serious look; that was good.

An old woman answered the door. She put on a coat and disappeared, then yelling something in Italian at the next room, she left the apartment.

Like the downstairs, it was very English, with big armchairs and thick carpets. Mi appeared in a short slip with bare legs and shoulders, a pencil in her mouth, and a lampshade in her hand. She explained that it had fallen off a lamp.

"How are you? Can you fix things? Come and see."

In a room that smelled of American cigarettes, with an unmade bed, Do fixed the lampshade without taking off her coat. Mi rummaged in a box on a dresser, then disappeared into another room. She returned with three ten-thousand-franc bills in one hand and a bath sponge in the other. She handed the money to Do, who took it mechanically, nonplussed.

"Is that enough?" asked Mi. "My God, I would never have known you, you know?"

She was looking at Do kindly, with beautiful attentive eyes, porcelain eyes. Up close, she was no more than twenty, and really very pretty. She stood still scarcely two seconds, then seemed to remember something urgent and rushed to the door.

"*Ciao*. Let me hear from you, promise?"

"But I don't understand . . ."

Do indicated the bills, following her. Mi wheeled around on the threshold of a bathroom where water was running.

"I don't want any money!" Do repeated.

"Isn't that what you said on the phone?"

"I said I wanted to talk to you."

Mi seemed genuinely sorry, or very much annoyed, or amazed, or all three.

"Talk to me? What about?"

"Oh, things," said Do. "Well, just see you and talk to you. That's all."

"At this hour? Listen, sit down, I have something to do, I'll be back in two minutes."

Do waited in the bedroom for half an hour, sitting in front of the bills she had put on the bed, not daring to take off her coat. Mi returned in a terry cloth robe, vigorously rubbing her wet hair with a towel. She said something in Italian which Do did not understand, then she asked:

"Do you mind if I get in bed? We'll talk for a minute. Do you live far from here? If no one will worry, you can sleep here if you like. There're heaps of beds, all over. Listen, I'm very glad to see you again, don't make such a face."

One wondered how she could pay attention to people's faces. She got in bed in her robe, lit a cigarette, told Do that if she wanted a drink, there were bottles in the next room somewhere. She fell asleep immediately, her lighted cigarette between her fingers, like a doll. Do could not believe her eyes. She touched her shoulder and the doll stirred, mumbled something, and dropped her cigarette on the floor.

"The cigarette," moaned Mi.

"I'm putting it out."

The doll made a kissing noise with her mouth and went back to sleep.

The next morning Do was late to the bank for the first time in two years. The old woman had waked her up without seeming surprised to find her lying on the couch. Mi had already left.

At lunch, in a bistro near the bank where they had a "special" every day, Do swallowed three cups of coffee. She was not hungry. She was as unhappy as if there had been an injustice. Life takes back with one hand what it gives you with the other: she had spent the night at Mi's, she had been admitted into her private life faster than she would ever have dared imagine, but she had even less excuse to see her again than she had the day before. Mi was unattainable.

When she left the bank that evening, Do ignored her date with Gabriel and returned to the Residence. They called apartment 14 from the lobby. Mlle. Isola was not in. Do spent the whole evening hanging around the Champs-Élysées, went to a movie, came back and walked under the windows of apartment 14. Around midnight, after again questioning a black-suited concierge, she gave up.

About ten days later, on a Wednesday morning, the *"coup de chance"* occurred a second time at the bank. Mi had on a turquoise outfit, for the weather was fair that day, and this time it was a boy who accompanied her. Do went up to her at the tellers' counter.

"I was just thinking of calling you," she said point-blank. "I found some old pictures, I wanted to ask you to have dinner and show them to you."

Mi, obviously surprised, said without conviction that that would be wonderful, they would have to make a date. She looked at Do attentively, as she had the night she had tried to give her money. Was she more interested in other people than she seemed? She must have read in

Do's eyes the entreaty, the hope, the fear of being rejected.

"Listen," she said, "I have to go to a boring party tomorrow evening, but I'll be through in time for dinner. Let me take you. Meet me somewhere around nine. At the Flore, if you like. I'm never late. *Ciao, carina.*"

The boy she was with favored Do with an indifferent smile. As they left the bank, he put his arm on the shoulder of the princess with the black hair.

She came into the Flore at two minutes to nine, her coat tossed over her shoulders, her face framed by a white scarf. Do, who had been sitting behind the glass partitions of the terrace for half an hour, had seen the MG go by a moment before and congratulated herself that Mi was alone.

Mi had a dry Martini, told about the gathering she had just left and a book she had finished the night before, paid, said she was dying of hunger, and asked whether Do liked Chinese restaurants.

They dined across from each other on rue Cujas and had different dishes, which they shared. Mi thought Do looked better with her hair down than she had with the bun she had worn the first evening. Hers was much longer, and a pain in the neck: two hundred strokes with the hairbrush every day. At times she regarded Do silently with an attention that was almost embarrassing. At other times, she kept up an inane monologue, as if it hardly mattered who was across from her.

"By the way, how about the pictures?"

"They're at my place," said Do. "It's near. I thought we might go there now."

As she got into the white MG, Mi announced that she felt good, that she was very pleased with the evening. She walked into the Hotel Victoria, remarking that it was a nice neighborhood, and she seemed immediately at home in Do's room. She took off her coat and shoes and curled up on the bed. They looked at little Mi and little Do and forgotten, nostalgic faces. Do, kneeling against her on the bed, wished this could go on forever. She smelled Mi's perfume so close to her that she would undoubtedly remain saturated with it after Mi left. She had slipped an arm around Mi's shoulders and she no longer knew whether it was her friend's warmth or her own that she felt. When Mi began to laugh at a picture of them together on the edge of a surfboard, Do could bear it no longer and desperately kissed her hair.

"Those were the days," said Mi.

She had not pulled away. She did not look at Do. There were no more pictures, but she did not move, probably a little embarrassed. At last, she turned her head and said very quickly, "Let's go to my place." She got up and put on her shoes. As Do did not follow, she came back and kneeled before her, placing her hand tenderly on Do's cheek.

"I want to be with you always," said Do.

And she drew against her forehead the shoulder of a little princess who was not indifferent, but sweet and vulnerable like the child she had once known, and who answered in a broken voice:

"You drank too much at that Chinese place, you don't know what you're saying."

In the MG, Do pretended to be interested in the Champs-Élysées which was going by outside the window. Mi did not talk. Apartment 14: the old woman was waiting, asleep in a chair. Mi dismissed her with two loud kisses on the cheeks, closed the door, flung her shoes across the room and her coat on a sofa. She was laughing, she seemed happy.

"What's your job like?" she asked.

"At the bank? Oh, it's too complicated to explain. And then, it's not interesting."

Mi, who had already pulled down the top of her dress, came back to Do and unbuttoned her coat.

"What a creep you are! Take that off, relax! You make me nervous like that. Move, will you?"

They wound up wrestling, falling together half on a chair, half on the carpet. Mi was the stronger; she laughed, caught her breath, holding Do by the wrists.

"So it's complicated, what you do? Yes, you look like a complicated girl. Since when are you a complicated girl? Since when do you make people nervous?"

"All my life," said Do. "I've never forgotten you. I've watched your windows for hours. I've imagined that I saved your life in a shipwreck. I've kissed your pictures."

Do could not go on. She was lying on the carpet, wrists pinned down, Mi on top of her.

"Well, what do you know," said Mi.

She got up and went into her bedroom. A moment later Do heard the water running in the bathroom. Later she got up too, went into Mi's room, and looked in the closet to see if she could find some pajamas or a nightgown. There was a pair of pajamas—in her size.

That night she slept on the sofa in the front room. Mi, in bed in the next room, chattered away, raising her voice to make herself heard. She had not taken any sleeping pills. She took them often, which explained why she had fallen asleep so suddenly the first night. Long after she had announced, " 'Night, Do!" she kept up her monologue.

About three o'clock in the morning, Do awoke and heard her crying. She hurried to her bedside and found her outside the bedclothes, in tears, sleeping with closed fists. She turned out the light, covered her up again, and went back to bed.

The next evening Mi had "someone" with her. From the Dupont-Latin where she was calling from, Do could hear this someone demanding his cigarettes. Mi answered, "On the table, right in front of your nose."

"Can't I see you?" said Do. "Who is that boy? Are you going out with him? Can't I see you afterward? I'll wait for you. I'll brush your hair. I'll do anything."

"You make me sick," said Mi.

At one o'clock the same night, she knocked on the door of Do's room at the Hotel Victoria. She must have drunk, smoked, and talked too much. She was depressed. Do undressed her, lent her a pajama top, put her in her own bed, and held her in her arms until the alarm went off, not sleeping, listening to her regular breathing, saying to herself, "It's not a dream now, she's here, she's mine, her perfume will be all over me when I leave her, I am her."

"Do you have to go down there?" asked Mi, opening one eye. "Come back to bed. I'll put you on 'The Register.' "

"The what?"

"My godmother's payroll. Come back to bed. I'll pay."

Do was dressed and ready to leave. She replied that it was ridiculous, she was not a plaything that is picked up and then forgotten. The bank paid her a salary every month, enough to live on. Mi sat up in bed, her face fresh and rested, her expression wide awake and angry.

"You talk like someone else I know. If I say I'll pay, I'll pay! What do they pay you at your bank?"

"Sixty-five thousand a month."

"You've got a raise," said Mi. "Come back to bed or I'll fire you."

Do took off her coat, put on some coffee, and looked out the window at a cloudless day. As she took the cup to the bed, she knew that her excitement would last more than one morning, and that from now on everything she did or said might someday be used against her.

"You're a nice plaything," said Mi. "You make good coffee. How long have you been living here?"

"A few months."

"Pack your bags."

"Mi, you've got to understand: it's serious, what you're making me do."

"Oh, I've known that for two days, believe me. Do you think there are many people who've saved me from a shipwreck? Besides, I'm sure you don't know how to swim."

"No."

"I'll teach you," said Mi. "It's easy. Look, you move your arms like this, see? The legs are harder . . ."

Laughing, she threw Do onto the bed and made her bend her arms. All at once she stopped, looked at Do without smiling, and said that she knew it was serious— but not that serious.

The next few nights Do slept on the couch in the front room of apartment 14, Residence Washington, watching, as it were, over the loves of Mi, who slept in the next room in the company of a rather conceited and disagreeable boy. He was the one she had seen at the bank. His name was Francois Roussin, he was secretary to a lawyer, and he was not unattractive. In a way he had the same vague ideas in mind as Do, and they frankly detested each other on sight.

Mi claimed he was good looking and harmless. At night, Do was too close not to hear her friend sighing in the arms of this ass. She suffered as if from jealousy, knowing it was a much simpler emotion. She was almost happy the night Mi asked her whether her room at the Hotel Victoria was still unoccupied: she wanted to spend the night there with another boy. The room was paid for until the end of March. Mi disappeared for three nights. Francois Roussin was very upset, but Do had nothing to fear from the other boy, about whom she knew nothing except that he was a racer, and who was very soon forgotten.

Then there were the nights when Mi was alone—the best nights. She could not stand to be alone. Someone to give her hair the two hundred strokes, someone to wash her back, someone to put out her cigarette if she fell asleep, someone to listen to her monologue: that was Do. She would suggest dinner for two and order up improbable dishes like scrambled eggs under silver covers. She would show Mi how to make animals by folding a napkin; every other word would be "love" or "pretty." Above all, she would put her hand on the nape of her neck or her shoulder, or her arm around her: she maintained a constant physical contact with Mi. This was the most important thing, considering her need to be consoled before she could sleep with pills, boys, or chatter, a need that was simply the ancient fear of the dark when Mama leaves the room. Mi's two most pronounced traits —pronounced to a degree that Do found pathological— came straight from infancy.

In March Do accompanied Mi—or Micky, as everyone called her—wherever she went, with the exception of Francois Roussin's apartment. This meant racing around Paris in the car from one store to another, from one visit to another, from a game of tennis on an indoor court to sitting around in restaurants with dull people. Do often stayed in the car, turning the dial of the radio or mentally drafting the letter she would write to Godmother Midola that night.

She wrote her first letter on the day she was "hired." In it she said that she had had the good fortune to find Mi again, that everything was fine, that she hoped the same was true for a godmother "who was almost her own." Then news of Nice, one or two carefully concealed digs at Micky, and a promise to come and give her a kiss on her first trip to Italy.

After she had sent the letter she had immediately regretted the digs. They were too obvious. Godmother Midola was shrewd; she must be, to have gone from the streets of Nice to an Italian *palazzo;* she would immediately be suspicious. Not at all: the answer came four days later, and she was fairly ecstatic. Do was a godsend. She had remained just as her Godmother Midola remembered her, sweet, sensible, affectionate. She must have noticed, though, that unfortunately "their" Micky had changed a great deal. It was to be hoped that this wonderful meeting would have a good influence, a check was enclosed.

Do returned the check with her second letter, promising to do all she could for "their" *enfant terrible,* who was merely very high-spirited, although at times it did seem that she had no heart, a thousand kisses, affectionately yours.

By the end of March Do had received her fifth reply. She was signing herself "Your god-daughter."

In April she found a clue. One evening while they were dining in a restaurant, she attacked Francois Roussin openly, in front of Micky, following some disagreement or other over her protégée's menu. The point was not that Micky slept poorly after a *coq au vin,* but that Francois was a rat, a parasite, a hypocrite, that she could not stand the sight of him.

Two nights later it was more serious. The restaurant was not the same, nor was the point of disagreement, but Francois was still a rat, and this time he lost his temper. Do heard herself accused of swindling, of emotional blackmail, of being a lesbian. At a final crude remark, Micky raised her hand. Do, who was waiting for the blow to land on her, felt she had scored a point when she saw it fall on the face of the rat.

She did not have long to wait. Back at the Residence, Francois made a scene, said he refused to spend the night in the company of an innocent and a voyeur. He left, slamming the door. The scene continued between Do, who defended herself by accusing him further, and Micky, who was wild with rage at hearing certain truths stated. It was not the make-believe fight of the first night; a shower of real blows, one after the other, forced Do across the room onto the bed, and back on her feet, brought forth tears and entreaties, and left her, disheveled, with a bloody nose, on her knees against a door. Micky pulled her to her feet and dragged her sobbing into the bathroom, and for once it was she who ran the water and got out the towels.

They did not speak to each other for three days. Francois came the next day. He examined Do's swollen face with a critical eye, said, "God, you're even uglier than usual," and took Micky out to celebrate. On the evening of the next day, Do took the hairbrush again and performed her "duty" without a word. The evening after that, since the silence was becoming ominous, she flung herself at Micky's knees and begged her forgiveness. They made up with tears and damp kisses, and Micky took out of her closet a pile of humiliating and pitiful presents. She had been shopping for three days to cheer herself up.

As ill luck would have it, that same week Do ran into Gabriel, whom she had not seen for a month. She was coming out of the hairdresser's. She still bore the marks of Micky's tantrum. Gabriel helped her into his Dauphine and pretended to have adjusted quite well to their separation. He was worried about her, that was all. He would worry even more after seeing her like this. What had happened to her? Do did not see any point in lying.

"She beat you up? And you take it?"

"I can't explain it to you. I'm happy with her. I need her like the air I breathe. You wouldn't understand. Men only understand men."

Gabriel shook his head, but dimly he guessed the truth. Do was trying to make him believe that she was infatuated with this cousin with the long hair. He knew Do: she was incapable of being infatuated with anyone. If she let herself be beaten by an hysterical girl, she must have something in mind, something mad, well thought out, and infinitely more dangerous.

"What have you been living on since you left the bank?"

"She gives me whatever I want."

"Where is this going to get you?"

"I have no idea. She isn't unkind, you know. She's very fond of me. I get up whenever I feel like it, I have clothes, I go with her wherever she goes. You can't understand."

She left him wondering whether on the contrary he had not understood quite well. But he was fond of her too. Everyone was fond of her, no one could read in her eyes that since the night she had been beaten, she felt as if she were dead, that it was not this spoiled child she needed, but a life she had lived too long in fantasy and that even the spoiled child did not lead. In her place, she would have known better how to take advantage of the luxury, the easy money, the dependence and cowardice of others. Micky would pay for her blows some day, as she had claimed she would pay for everything. But more important still, she was going to have to pay for the illusions of a little bank employee who depended on no one, asked love from no one, and did not believe the world revolved around her.

For several days now Do had had a premonition that she was going to kill Mi. On the sidewalk, after she had left Gabriel, she told herself simply that she had one more reason. Not only would she be doing away with a useless insect, a creature of no consequence, but with her own humiliation and resentment. She looked for her dark glasses in her handbag: first, because people can actually read these things in your face; next, because she had a bruise under one eye.

In May Micky went a little too far. She listened to some wild ideas of Francois Roussin's and decided to move into a private hotel which Godmother Midola owned in rue de Courcelles. La Raffermi had never lived there. Micky threw herself into the project with a vengeance. Since she was determined to go ahead with it but had no credit except for her aunt's, communications between Paris and Florence broke down in forty-eight hours.

Micky got the money she needed to cover her signatures, commissioned the painters and the furniture, but Francois Chance was assigned as a go-between and the alarm was sounded to summon a first-class monster, a vicious and legendary creature, since she was said to have given Micky spankings.

The monster's name was Jeanne Murneau. Micky spoke of her seldom and in such vile terms that it was easy to imagine how afraid she was of her. To take down Micky's pants and smack her on the buttocks, even at the age of fourteen, as it had happened, was in itself a feat. But to say "no" when Micky, now twenty, was saying "yes," and to make her listen to reason, this belonged to the realm of legend; it was inconceivable.

This was not an altogether true picture, however, as Do realized as soon as she saw the monster. She was tall, blond, and even-tempered. Micky was not afraid of her, did not hate her; it was worse: she could not endure her presence. Her adoration was so total, her nervousness so apparent that it gave Do a queer feeling. Perhaps bank employees were not the only ones who cried into their pillows. For years Micky had obviously been imagining a Murneau who did not exist, from whom she suffered without rhyme or reason; she went crazy when Jeanne was around. Do, who had heard the monster mentioned only in passing, was astounded at her importance.

It was an evening like any other. Micky was changing to meet Francois. Do was reading in an armchair; it was she who answered the door. Jeanne Murneau looked at her as if she were a loaded revolver, took off her coat, and called without raising her voice, "Micky, are you coming?"

The girl appeared in a bathrobe, trying to smile. She looked as if she had been caught red-handed; her lips were trembling. There was a short exchange in Italian of which Do understood only that Micky was letting herself be torn apart phrase by phrase, like a piece of frayed knitting. She shifted from one foot to the other, unrecognizable.

Jeanne strode toward her and kissed her on the temple, holding her by the elbows, and then stared at her for a long time. What she was saying must not be very pleasant. The voice was low and calm, but the tone was sharp as a whip. Micky tossed her long hair and did not answer. Finally Do saw her go pale, tear her arms from the monster's grasp, and pull away, drawing her robe together.

"I didn't ask you to come here! Why didn't you stay where you were? I haven't changed and neither have you. You're still Murneau the Bloody Nuisance; only now I have my claque."

"You are Domenica?" asked Jeanne, suddenly turning around. "Go and turn off the water."

"You'll move when I say so!" Micky put in, blocking Do's way. "Stay where you are. If you listen to that woman once, you'll never get rid of her."

Do found that she had unconsciously moved back three steps. Jeanne shrugged her shoulders and went into the bathroom to shut the water off herself. When she returned, Micky had pushed Do into a chair and was standing beside her. Her lips were still trembling.

Jeanne paused on the threshold, a big girl with blond hair who emphasized her remarks with an outstretched finger and spoke at top speed to avoid being interrupted. Do heard her name spoken several times.

"Speak French," said Micky. "Do doesn't understand. You're dying of jealousy. She'd be amazed if she understood. No, but look at you, you're dying of jealousy! If you could see yourself! You're disgusting, you know, really disgusting."

Jeanne smiled and answered that this had nothing to do with Do, that if Do would go out of the room for a few minutes, it would be better for everyone.

"Do stays where she is!" said Micky. "She understands very well. She's listening to me, she isn't listening to you. I love her, she's mine. Look at this."

Micky leaned over, pulled Do toward her with a hand on the back of her neck, and kissed her on the mouth once, twice, three times. Do submitted, breathless, paralyzed, saying to herself, "I'll kill her, I'll find a way to kill her, but who is this Italian to drive her to such limits?" Micky's lips were sweet and trembling.

"When you've finished your little act," said Jeanne Murneau in a calm voice, "get dressed and pack your bag. La Raffermi wants to see you."

Micky straightened up, of the three women the most ill at ease, and looked around for a suitcase. There was one in the room, she had seen it a moment ago. Where had it gone? It was on the rug behind her, open, empty.

She seized it in both hands and threw it at Jeanne Murneau, who ducked it.

Micky took two steps, screaming something in Italian, probably an insult, grabbed a pretty blue vase from the mantelpiece and threw it as well at the big blond girl's head. Jeanne dodged everything without moving an inch. The vase smashed to pieces against a wall. Jeanne strode around a table and over to Micky, took her by the chin with one hand and slapped her with the other.

Then she put her coat back on, said that she was spending the night at rue de Courcelles and leaving at noon the next day, and that she had an airplane ticket for Micky. At the door, she added that La Raffermi was dying. She had no more than ten days to live. When she was gone, Micky fell into a chair and burst into tears.

Do rang the doorbell at rue de Courcelles just as Mi and Francois must have been entering the theater. Jeanne Murneau was not particularly surprised to see her. She took her coat and hung it on a doorknob. The house was full of ladders, paint cans, and torn paper.

"All the same, she does have taste," said Murneau. "It's going to be very pretty. The paint makes my head ache, doesn't it yours? Come upstairs, it's more habitable."

Upstairs, in a partially decorated room, they sat side by side on the edge of a bed.

"Do you want to talk or shall I?" asked Jeanne.

"Go ahead."

"I'm thirty-five. This nuisance was wished on me seven years ago. I'm not proud of what she's become, but I wasn't any prouder when I got her. You were born July 4, 1939. You worked in a bank. On February 18 of this year you looked at Micky with your big brown eyes, after which you changed your profession. You have become a sort of doll who takes slaps and kisses without batting an eye. You seem like a nice girl, you're prettier than I expected, but just as tiresome. You have an idea in your head and ordinarily dolls don't have ideas."

"I don't know what you're talking about."

"Then let me continue. You have had an idea in your head for a thousand years. It's not really an idea, but something vague and indefinite like an itch. Many other people have felt it before you, myself for one, but you're by all odds the stupidest and most determined. I want you to understand me from the start: it's not the idea that bothers me, but the fact that you carry it like a flag. You've already made enough mistakes to rouse the suspicions of twenty people. When these people are as limited as Francois Roussin, you'll admit it's serious. La Raffermi is all right, but she has a cool head. As for taking Micky for a fool, that's madness. You're not using your head, and you annoy me."

"I still don't understand," said Do. Her throat was dry; she told herself it was the smell of paint. She tried to get up, but the tall girl with the golden hair calmly restrained her.

"I've read your letters to La Raffermi."

"She showed them to you?"

"You're living in a dream. I've seen them, that's all. And the report attached to them: brunette, five feet six inches, born in Nice, father an accountant, mother a housekeeper, two lovers, one at eighteen, for three months, one at twenty until the arrival of Micky, 65,000 francs per month less social security, distinguishing characteristic: stupid."

Do broke away and made for the door. On the first floor she could not find her coat. Jeanne Murneau reappeared and handed it to her.

"Don't be childish. I need to talk to you. Surely you haven't had dinner. Come with me."

In the taxi Jeanne Murneau gave the address of a restaurant near the Champs-Élysées. When they were sitting across the table from each other Do noticed that her gestures were very much like Micky's, but they seemed caricatured because she was so much taller. Jeanne intercepted her look and said in an irritated voice, as if it were only too easy to read her mind, "She is the imitator, not I. What do you want to eat?"

All through the meal she kept her head a little to one side and one elbow on the table, like Micky. When she spoke she often extended her large, fine hand, or pointed her finger like a schoolteacher. This, in exaggerated form, was also a gesture of Micky's.

"It's your turn to talk, you know."

"I have nothing to say to you."

"Then why did you come to see me?"

"To explain. It doesn't matter now, you don't trust me."

"To explain what?"

"That Micky loves you very much, that she cried after you left, that you are too hard on her."

"Really? I mean, did you really come to tell me that? You see, there's something I didn't know before I met you which I'm beginning to understand: you're a terrible hypocrite. You can't take people for such fools."

"I still don't know what you're talking about."

"Mama Raffermi understood, believe me, you little

fool! And Micky is a hundred times smarter than you are! If you don't understand, I'll draw you a picture. You're counting on an imaginary Micky, not the real one. For the moment, it's love at first sight, she's a little blinded by it. But the way you're going, you won't even last as long as her other fads. There's something worse: when Raffermi got your letters, she didn't make a move. Those letters! They're enough to make your hair stand on end! And I assume she answers you nicely. Didn't that seem strange to you?"

"My letters, my letters! What's wrong with my letters?"

"They have one fault: they're all about you. 'How I'd like to be Micky, how you'd appreciate me if I were in her place, how I'd be able to take advantage of the life you offer her!' Isn't that so?"

Do put her head in her hands.

"There are certain things you must know," continued Jeanne Murneau. "Your best chance is to please Micky, for a thousand reasons you don't understand. And to be there at the right moment. Then, you'll never be able to come between Micky and Raffermi. You don't understand that either, but that's the way it is. Not worth getting excited about. Finally, Raffermi has had three attacks in forty-five days. In a week, a month, she'll be dead. Your letters are useless and dangerous. Micky will be left, and that's all there is to it."

Jeanne Murneau, who had eaten nothing, pushed her plate away, took an Italian cigarette from a pack sitting on the table, and added, "And myself, of course."

They walked back to the Residence. They did not talk. The tall blond girl held her arm. When they reached the corner of rue Lord Byron, Do stopped and said very fast, "I'll come with you, I don't feel like going in."

They got into a taxi. At rue de Courcelles, the paint smell seemed stronger. As they entered a room, Jeanne Murneau kept Do from walking under a ladder. She took her by the shoulders in the dark, and made her stand up straight, even lifting her a little on tiptoe, as if to bring her up to her own height.

"You are to keep calm. No more letters, no more fights with anyone, no more nonsense. In a few days you'll move in here, the two of you. La Raffermi will be dead. I'll ask Micky to come to Florence. I'll ask her in such a way that she won't come. As for Francois, you'll wait for me to provide you with a good argument. When that happens, there won't be a moment to lose, get rid of Francois and get Micky away from him. The argument will be airtight. I'll tell you where to take her. Did you understand this time? Are you listening to me?"

In the shaft of moonlight falling through the window, Do nodded her head. The large hands of the girl with the golden eyes were still gripping her shoulders. Do no longer tried to pull away.

"All you have to do is keep calm. Don't take Micky for a fool; I did it before you and I was wrong. I looked at her one night the way I'm looking at you now; it was the biggest mistake of my life. She was sixteen, almost as old as I was when Raffermi took me in, almost as old as you are now. I know you only through your letters, which are ridiculous, but I would have written them myself once. When they saddled me with Micky, I would gladly have drowned her. My feelings have not changed since then. But I won't drown her, I have another way to get rid of her: you. A little idiot who trembles but who will do what I tell her, because she wants to get rid of her too."

"Let me go, please."

"Listen to me. Before Micky, there was another girl like her with Raffermi—a few inches taller, and eighteen years old. It was me. I used to paint the heels of shoes with a little paintbrush, in Florence. Then, everything I wanted was given to me. And then, it was taken away again: Micky was there. I want you to think about that, and keep calm. Everything you feel, I have felt. But I have learned a few things since then. Will you think about that? Now you may go."

Do was led to the front hallway in the dark. She stumbled over a paint can. A door opened before her. She turned around, but the tall girl pushed her out without a word and closed the door after her.

At noon the next day when Do called Jeanne from a café on the Champs-Élysées, she had left. The ring of the telephone must be echoing from room to room in an empty house.

I MURDERED

MY WHITE-GLOVED HAND covered her mouth. She drew it away gently and rose, a long silhouette on the rectangle of light from the next room. One night we had already been like this in the half-light, she and I. She had held me by the shoulders. She had suggested that I murder a princess with long hair.

"How do you know all this? There are some things you can't know: the night she slept at my hotel, the night I hung around under her windows. And then the time I met that boy, Gabriel . . ."

"You told me about it yourself!" said Jeanne. "We spent two weeks together in June."

"Didn't you see Micky again after the fight at the Residence?"

"No. I didn't care. I wasn't at all anxious to take her back to Italy. The next morning I saw Francois Chance to settle the matter of the decorating, and caught my plane. When I got back to Florence, I had my problems. La Raffermi was beside herself with rage. I wouldn't swear that Micky hadn't telephoned her after she saw me. You always maintained she hadn't. In any case, it didn't do any good. Raffermi stayed mad to the end."

"When did she die?"

"A week later."

"And you said nothing more to me before you left?"

"No. I had nothing more to say. You knew very well what I meant. Long before you met me, you thought of nothing else."

All of a sudden there was light in the room; she had turned on a lamp. I covered my eyes with my gloved hand.

"Turn it out, please!"

"Do you mind if I worry about you? Do you know what time it is? You're dead tired. I've brought you some gloves. Take off the ones you have on."

While she was bending over my hands, tall, blond, considerate, all that she had told me seemed again like a bad dream. She was generous and good, and I was incapable of planning Micky's death—none of it was true.

Soon it was dawn. She took me in her arms and carried me up to the second floor. In the hall, as she came near Do's old room, I could only shake my head against her cheek. She understood and laid me down on her own bed, in the room she had stayed in while I was at the clinic. A moment later, after she had taken off my bathrobe and given me something to drink, she bent over me as I shivered under the covers, tucked me in, and con-templated my face silently with tired eyes.

Downstairs, at some forgotten point in her story, I had told her that I wanted to die. Now, feeling drowsi-ness overcome me, I was seized by an absurd fear.

"What did you give me to drink?"

"Water, with two sleeping capsules."

She must have read my mind, as usual, for she put her hand over my eyes. I heard her saying, "You're mad, mad, mad, mad," and her voice rapidly became fainter, I could no longer feel her hand on my face, then all of a sudden, a smiling American soldier with his cap on crooked handed me a chocolate bar, the teacher came toward me with a ruler to rap my hands, and I fell asleep.

In the morning I stayed in bed and Jeanne lay beside me on the covers, fully dressed. We decided to live at rue de Courcelles from now on. She told me the story of the murder and I told her about my inquiries of the day before. It now seemed altogether inconceivable to me that Francois had not revealed the substitution.

"It's not that simple," said Jeanne. "Physically you're no longer either yourself or Micky. I don't mean just your face, but the impression you give. You don't walk the way she did, but you don't walk the way *you* did either. And then, you lived with her for several months. During the last weeks you watched her so closely, to be able to imitate her, that I see it in all your movements. When you laughed the first evening, I no longer knew who it was. The worst part was that I couldn't remember what she was like, or what you were like, I lost the ability to reason. You'll never know the things I imagined.

When I gave you your bath, I thought I'd gone back four years in time, because you're thinner than Micky, and she used to be something like that. At the same time I told myself it was impossible, you were the same size, but you didn't look anything alike. I couldn't make that big a mistake. I was afraid you were putting on an act for my benefit."

"Why?"

"As if I knew! To get rid of me, to be alone. What was driving me crazy was that *I couldn't speak to you until you knew*. I was the one who had to put on an act. By treating you as if you really were she, I got confused. I realized something terrible in those four days, but something that will make things easier for us: as soon as I heard your voice, I couldn't remember Micky's; as soon as I saw your beauty spot, Micky had always had it, or you had always had it—I no longer knew. One doesn't remember, do you understand? Suddenly you would make a gesture, and I would see Micky again. I would think about this gesture so much that I would succeed in convincing myself I'd made a mistake. The truth is that you really did make a gesture of Micky's, between two of your own, because for weeks you said to yourself, Some day I'll have to do it exactly like that."

"Would that be enough to deceive Francois? It's not possible. I spent half a day with him. At first he didn't recognize me, but in the evening we were on a couch, he kissed me and tried to make love to me for over an hour."

"You *were* Mi. He was talking about Mi. He believed he was with Mi. And then, he's a gold-digger; he never paid attention to her, he was sleeping with an inheritance. You won't see him again, that's all. I'm much more concerned about your visit with Francois Chance."

"He didn't notice anything."

"I won't give him a chance to notice anything. Now we're really going to get down to work."

She said that when we returned to Florence the risks would be much greater. There they had known Mi for years. In Nice there was only Mi's father to worry about. Suddenly I realized that I would have to see this man whose daughter I had killed, fall into his arms as she would have done. In Nice, too, my mother and father were still mourning their lost daughter; they would undoubtedly want to see me so I would tell them about her, they would look at me with horror—they would recognize me!

"Don't talk nonsense!" cried Jeanne, gripping my forearms. "You won't have to see them! Micky's father, you'll have to see him. If you cry a little, they'll put it down to the emotion. But it'd be best from now on if you didn't think about your parents again. Do you even remember them?"

"No. But when I do remember?"

"By then you'll be another person. You are another person: you're Micky. Michele Marthe Sandra Isola, born November 14, 1939. You're four months younger, you've lost your fingerprints and grown an inch. That's all there is to it."

It was only the beginning of a new anxiety. At noon she went to the house in Neuilly to pack up our things. She brought them back, the clothes thrown every which way in our bags. I went down into the garden in my bathrobe to help her bring them in. She sent me away, telling me I would "catch my death."

Everything either of us said took me bac[k]
again to that night at Cap Cadet that she [k]
about. I did not want to think about it, I co[uld]
the thought of seeing some movies of Mi[cky]
taken on a holiday, which might help me imitate her.
But the least word took on a double meaning and called
up images more unbearable than any movie.

She dressed me and made me eat lunch. She said she
was sorry to have to leave me alone for two hours, but
she had to see Francois Chance and undo the damage I
had done the day before.

I got through the afternoon, dragging myself from
one chair to another. I looked at myself in the mirrors.
I took off my gloves and looked at my hands. In terror
and despair I observed this person who was becoming
me, a person who was nothing but words and confused
ideas.

More distressing to me than the crime I had committed
was this sensation of coming under an influence. I was a
hollow plaything, a puppet in the hands of three unknown women. Which of them was pulling the strings
the hardest? The envious little bank employee, patient
as a spider? The dead princess who would eventually
look back into my eyes from my mirror, since it was she
I wanted to become? Or the tall girl with the golden hair
who had led me to the murder for weeks without seeing
me?

After Godmother Midola died, Jeanne told me, Micky
refused to go to Florence. The funeral had taken place
without her, and they did not even bother to make an
excuse to La Raffermi's intimates.

The night she learned of the decease, Micky decided to go out with Francois and some friends. I went with her. Micky got drunk and made a scene in a night club on the Étoile, insulted the men who threw us out, and wanted to take home another boy besides Francois. She persisted and Francois had to go to his own place.

Finally, an hour after Francois' departure, the boy was also asked to leave, and I had to stay up half the night with her. She cried, talked about her dead mother and her childhood, said that she had lost Jeanne forever, and did not want to hear about her or anyone else again, that some day I would understand "what it's all about." Sleeping pill.

For several days she was much in demand. People felt sorry for her. She was invited everywhere. She behaved herself and carried the millions Raffermi had left her with dignity. She moved into rue de Courcelles as soon as it was habitable, even before the work was completed.

One afternoon when I was alone in our new quarters, I received a telegram from Jeanne. It consisted of her name and a telephone number in Florence. I called immediately. The first thing she said was that I was crazy to call from Micky's, then that it was time to get rid of Francois. As if the idea had occurred to me spontaneously, I was to ask Micky to check the estimates for rue de Courcelles and see what kind of arrangements her lover had made with the decorators. She asked me to call her again at the same number exactly a week later. This time it would be better to call from a post office.

Micky made her inquiries the next day, saw the decorators and, as she thought, discovered nothing irregular in the accounts. I wondered what Jeanne had in mind.

Obviously Francois' thinking went much further than a commission on some paintings or furniture, and the idea of cheating Micky in such an obvious way would not have occurred to him.

I realized that there was no question of this when I saw the scene he was subjected to after we got home. He had been personally responsible for everything. Copies of the estimates and invoices had been sent to Florence even before Micky had mentioned her plans. Francois defended himself as well as he could: he worked for Chance, it was natural that he should be in correspondence with Raffermi. Micky called him a boot-licker, a stool pigeon, and a gold-digger, and threw him out.

She would certainly have seen him again the next day, but now I knew what Jeanne wanted: I had only to take advantage of the momentum she had given me. Micky went to see Chance, who knew nothing about the matter. She called a secretary of Raffermi's in Florence and learned that in the hope of getting into her good graces, Francois had kept Godmother Midola informed of everything. The most comical part was that he also returned the checks that were sent to him.

I called Jeanne as had been agreed. It was the end of May. The weather was wonderful in Paris, and even better in the south. She told me to use my influence with Micky and talk her into bringing me down there. La Raffermi had a villa on the seashore, the place was called Cap Cadet. We would meet there when the time came.

"The time for what?"

"Hang up," said Jeanne. "I'll do whatever's necessary to help you persuade her. You just be nice and let me do the thinking. Call me again in a week. I hope you'll be ready to leave."

"Haven't they opened the will? Are there any problems? Might I ask . . ."

"Hang up," said Jeanne. "You bore me."

Ten days later, in early June, Micky and I were at Cap Cadet. We drove all night in her little car loaded with bags. In the morning a local woman named Yvette who knew "Murneau" opened the villa for us.

It was huge, sunny, and smelled of pines. We went down to take a swim on a deserted pebble beach at the foot of the promontory dominated by the house. Micky started to teach me how to swim. We fell onto a bed in damp bathing suits and slept side by side until evening.

I awoke first. For a long time I watched Micky sleeping against me, I imagined I know not what dreams behind her long lowered lashes, I touched a leg that was warm and alive, and pushed it away from mine. I was horrified at myself. I took the car and went to La Ciotat, the nearest town. I called Jeanne and told her I was horrified at myself.

"Then go back where you came from. Find another bank. Take in washing like your mother. Leave me alone."

"If you were here it wouldn't be this way. Why don't you come?"

"Where are you calling from?"

"The post office."

"Then listen carefully. I'm sending you a telegram in care of Micky, at the Café de la Desirade, La Ciotat. It's the last one at the end of the beach, before you turn left to go back to Cap Cadet. Let them know casually that you're expecting it, and go pick it up tomorrow morning. Then call me. Now hang up."

I stopped at the café, ordered a Coca Cola, and asked

the owner to keep any mail he got addressed to Isola. He asked me whether it was love or business. Since it was love, he agreed.

, That night Micky was depressed. After the dinner Mme. Yvette served us, we took her back to Les Lecques, where she lived, strapping her bicycle to the back of the MG. Then Micky decided to go on to more civilized places, drove me to Bandol, danced until two o'clock in the morning, found the southern boys boring, and took me home. She chose a room for herself and for me, kissed me on the cheek sleepily, and left me with the promise that "we certainly weren't going to rot in this hole." I wanted to see Italy, she had promised to take me there, she was going to show me the Bay of Naples, Castellammare, Sorrento, Amalfi. They were terrific. Good night, sweetie.

Late the next morning, I stopped at the Café de la Desirade. Jeanne's telegram was incomprehensible: "Clarissa coupling. Fondly." I called Florence again from the La Ciotat post office.

"She doesn't like it here. She wants to take me to Italy."

"She can't have very much money," said Jeanne. "She doesn't know anyone, she'll be in touch with me before long. Until then I can't come, she wouldn't stand for it. Did you get my message?"

"Yes, but I don't understand it."

"I didn't expect you to. I was referring to the second floor, the first door on the right. I advise you to look around and think about what you see. Thinking is always better than talking, especially on the telephone. Unscrew, and moisten every day, that's all you have to do. Hang up and think. Of course there's no question of your coming to Italy."

I heard some buzzing in the receiver, a muffled chorus of voices between La Ciotat and Florence, relaying the call from one operator to the next. Of course one listener was enough, but what would she have heard that was so disturbing?

"Must I call you again?"

"In a week. Be careful."

I went into the bathroom adjoining my room in the late afternoon, while Micky was lying on the beach. "Clarissa" was the trademark on the water heater. The pipe must have been installed recently, it was unpainted. It ran all around the room at the top of the walls. I found the coupling at the mouth of an elbow. To get at it, I had to go and get a monkey wrench from the garage. I took the one that was in the tool kit in the car. Mme. Yvette was polishing the tiles on the ground floor. She was talkative and made me lose several minutes. When I got back to the bathroom, I was afraid Micky would come in unexpectedly. I jumped every time Mme. Yvette moved a chair downstairs.

Nevertheless I unscrewed the coupling nut and removed the coupling. In it was a thick plate of a substance resembling cardboard. I replaced it, screwed the coupling nut back to where I had found it, turned the gas back on, and relighted the pilot of the water heater which I had extinguished.

Micky appeared at the top of the path leading to the beach just as I was putting the monkey wrench back into the tool kit.

Jeanne's plan was only half clear to me. I understood that moistening the cardboard plate every day was meant to break it down slowly, almost naturally. The dampness would be attributed to the steam from the baths we took.

I decided to increase these baths so as to leave marks on the ceiling and walls. But what good would this do? If Jeanne wanted me to put a gas pipe out of order, it meant that she was planning to start a fire. If gas were to escape through the pipe, the pilot light would cause an explosion—but there would never be enough gas escaping from the pipe, the nut would hold it in.

Even if Jeanne's plan were better conceived than this and the fire were possible, what good would it do us? With Micky out of the way, I would also be cut off from the life I was leading, I would be back where I started. For a week I did as Jeanne had asked without having the courage to understand it. I dipped the plate in water, I weakened it little by little with my fingers, and I felt my resolution weakening along with it.

"I don't see what you expect to get out of this," I said to Jeanne over the telephone. "Now, listen: either you come here at once, or I forget the whole thing."

"Have you done what I told you to do?"

"Yes, but I want to know what comes next. I don't see what's in this for you, and I *know* there's nothing in it for me."

"Don't talk nonsense. How is Micky?"

"Fine. She's at the beach. We bowl in the swimming pool. They haven't been able to fill it. They don't know how it works. We take walks."

"Boys?"

"Not one. I hold her hand till she goes to sleep. She says she's through with love anyway. When she's had a little to drink, she talks about you."

"Can you talk like Micky?"

I did not understand the question.

"This is your reason for going on, darling. Do you

understand? No? Never mind. Well, go on, talk like Micky, imitate her, so I can hear a little of her."

"You call this living? First of all, Jeanne's out of her mind. Do you know what her sign is? Taurus. Look out for Taurus, sweetie, they've got the hide of an elephant. Everything in the head and nothing in the heart. What's your sign, dear? Cancer, not bad. You have the eyes for it. I used to know someone with eyes like that, great big ones like this, look. It was funny, you know. Jeanne? I feel sorry for her, poor girl. She's four inches too tall to let herself go. Do you know what she dreams about?"

"That's enough," said Jeanne. "I don't want to know."

"It's interesting, though; but it is hard to say over the telephone. Well, is that all right?"

"No. You're repeating, you're not making it up. Supposing you had to make it up? Think about that. I'll join you in a week, as soon as she gets in touch with me."

"You'd better bring along some good arguments. I've been told to think so many times, I'm thinking."

In the car that evening, on the way to Bandol where she wanted to have dinner, Micky told me that she had met a strange boy that afternoon. A strange boy with strange ideas. She looked at me and added that she was going to have fun in this place after all.

She did not keep me informed of her financial difficulties. When I needed money, I asked her for it. The next day, without telling me why, she stopped the car in front of the La Ciotat post office. We went in together, me half dead with fear to find myself in this place with her. An employee even asked me, "Is it for Florence?"

Fortunately Micky paid no attention, or thought the question was meant for her. As it turned out, she wanted to send a telegram to Florence. She had fun composing it. She showed it to me, and I saw that she was asking for money, that Jeanne would soon be here. It was the famous telegram of the "eyes, hands, mouth, be nice."

Jeanne arrived three days later on the seventeenth of June, in her white Fiat, a scarf over her blond head. Night was falling. The villa was full of people, boys and girls Micky had met on a near-by beach and brought home with her. I ran to meet Jeanne, who was parking her car. She merely handed me one of her bags and led the way to the house.

Her arrival was first a signal for silence, then for disbanding. In the garden, without a word to Jeanne, Micky bade everyone a tragic adieu, begging them to return when times were better. She was drunk and overstimulated. Jeanne, who seemed younger in a summer dress, was already straightening up the rooms.

Micky came back and fell into a chair with a glass in her hand. She ordered me to stop playing maid—I was helping Jeanne—and reminded me that she had already warned me that if I listened once to that beanpole, I'd never hear the end of it.

Then to Jeanne, "I asked for money, not for you. Give me the check, sleep here if you like, but be out of here tomorrow."

Jeanne went over to her and gave her a long look. Then she reached down, picked her up, and took her to the bathroom and put her under the shower. Later, she found me sitting on the edge of the swimming pool. She said that Micky was quiet and that we were going for a drive.

I got into her car. We stopped in a pine woods between Cap Cadet and Les Lecques.

"July 4 is your birthday," said Jeanne. "You'll go out

115

for dinner and have a little celebration together, that will look natural afterward. That's the night it will happen. How is the plate?"

"It's all spongy, like papier-mâché. But your plan is crazy: the nut won't let the gas out."

"The nut that'll be on the pipe that night will, idiot! I have another nut, the same kind, from the same plumber. It's broken, and completely rusted on the broken edge. Listen to me, will you? The fire, the investigation, the experts, these don't worry me. The installation was done this year, they'll find a defective nut, one that's been rusty for the right length of time. The house is insured against accidents: I took care of that, and I knew what I was doing when I chose it. Even the insurance company won't bother us. The only problem is you."

"Me?"

"How will you be able to take her place?"

"I thought you had a plan for that too. I mean, besides the one I'm thinking of."

"That's the only one there is."

"Would I have to do it alone?"

"If I am involved in the fire, they won't believe me when I identify you. But I must be the first one to identify you. Besides, what are they going to think if I'm here?"

"I don't know."

"It won't take them forty-eight hours to discover everything. If the two of you are alone, if you do exactly what I tell you to do, no questions will be asked."

"Would I have to hit Micky?"

"Micky will be drunk. You'll give her one more sleeping capsule than usual. Since afterward Micky will be you and there will undoubtedly be an autopsy, see to it, starting now, that everyone knows you take sleeping pills. And on that day, eat what she eats and drink what she drinks if there are witnesses."

"And would I have to burn myself?"

Had Jeanne drawn my head against her cheek just then to comfort me? When she related the scene to me, she claimed that she had, that it was then that she had started to care for me.

"That's the only problem. If I find you even slightly recognizable, we're both done for, there'd be no point in going on because I would identify you as Do."

"I'll never be able to do it."

"Yes you will. I swear to you that if you do as I say, it won't last more than five seconds. After that, you won't feel anything. I'll be there when you wake up."

"Who wouldn't be recognizable? How can I be sure I won't die too?"

"The face and the hands," said Jeanne. "Five seconds between the time you feel the fire and the time you're out of danger."

I had been able. Jeanne had stayed with us two weeks. The day before July 1, she said she had to make a business trip to Nice. I had been able to spend three days alone with Micky. I had been able to continue acting naturally. I had been able to go through with it.

On the night of July 4 the MG was seen in Bandol. Micky was seen getting drunk with her friend Domenica, in the company of half a dozen young people they had run into. At one o'clock in the morning the little white car was speeding toward Cap Cadet with Domenica at the wheel.

An hour later one side of the villa was in flames, the

side of the garage and Domenica's bathroom. A girl of twenty was burned alive in the next room, a girl wearing pajamas and a ring on her right hand which permitted her to be identified as me. The other girl was unable to rescue her from the flames, but gave the impression of having tried to save her. On the ground floor, to which the fire had spread, she performed her last doll-like gestures. She set fire to a wad of material, a nightgown of Micky's, took it in her hands, howling, and covered her face with it. Five seconds later, all was indeed over. She had collapsed at the foot of a stairway before she could reach a swimming pool which was no longer used for bowling and whose water rippled nearer and nearer beneath the sparks.

I had been able to do it.

"What time did you first get back to the villa?"

"Around ten o'clock," said Jeanne. "You had left for dinner long since. I changed the nut and turned the pilot on without lighting it. When you went upstairs all you had to do was throw a bit of burning cotton into the room. You were to do this after giving Micky the sleeping pills. I assume this is what you did."

"Where were you?"

"I went back to Toulon in order to be seen. I went into a restaurant and said that I was coming back from Nice, and on my way to Cap Cadet. When I got back to the villa, it was not burning. It was two o'clock in the morning; I realized that you were behind schedule. We had anticipated that by two it would all be over. But Micky must have created some difficulties about going home, I don't know. You were supposed to be taken suddenly ill. She was supposed to have driven you back at one. Something went wrong, because you were driving the car on the way back. Unless there was some mistake, I don't know."

"What did you do?"

"I waited on the road. At about two-fifteen I saw the first flames. I waited a little longer. I didn't want to be the first to arrive on the premises. When I picked you up on the stairs in front of the house, there were half a dozen people in pajamas and bathrobes who didn't know what to do. The firemen from Les Lecques arrived next and put out the fire."

"Was it part of the plan that I would try to get her out of my room?"

"No. It was not such a bad idea, for the inspectors from Marseille were quite impressed by it. But it was dangerous. And I think that was why you were black from head to foot. At the last minute you must have gotten trapped in the room and jumped out the window. You were supposed to have set fire to the night-gown on the ground floor. We had counted a hundred times to see how many steps it would take you to get to the swimming pool: seventeen. You were also supposed to wait to set fire to the nightgown until the neighbors were coming, so you'd fall into the pool just as they got there. Apparently you didn't wait. In the end you may have been afraid they wouldn't fish you out in time, and you didn't jump into the pool."

"I might have passed out immediately when I covered my head, and not been able to go any farther."

"I don't know. The wound you had on the top of your head was very large and very deep. Dr. Chaveres thinks you jumped from the second floor."

"With that nightgown around my head, if I didn't reach the swimming pool, I could have died! Your plan was strange, you know."

"No. We burned four nightgowns just like it. It never took more than seven seconds, without a draft. You were supposed to get to the swimming pool in seventeen steps. Five seconds, or even seven seconds, only on the hands and face, could not kill you. That wound on the head was not part of the plan, any more than the burns you had on your body."

"Could I have acted differently from the plan? Why wouldn't I have followed your instructions right to the end?"

"I'm telling you what happened in my own way," said Jeanne. "Perhaps it was not so easy for you to do as I said. It was more complicated. You were afraid of what you would have to do, afraid of the consequences, afraid of me. At the last minute, I think you decided to improve on the plan. They found her at the door of the room, she was supposed to have been in her bed, or near her bed. Perhaps for a moment you really wanted to save her; I don't know."

For ten or fifteen days, during this month of October, every night I had the same dream: I was trying with very rapid but completely ineffectual movements to rescue a girl with long hair from fire, from drowning, from being run over by a huge, driverless vehicle. I woke in a cold sweat, knowing myself for a coward: enough of a coward to drug an unhappy girl and burn her alive; too much of a coward to deny myself this lie of having tried to save her. The amnesia was an escape. If I could not remember who I was it was because not for the world, poor thing, could I have endured that memory.

We stayed in Paris until the end of October. I saw the movies of Micky's vacation twenty, thirty times. I learned her gestures, her walk, her way of turning her eyes abruptly toward the camera, toward me.

"She had the same abruptness in her speech," Jeanne told me. "You speak too slowly. She always started a new sentence before finishing the one that went before. She jumped from one idea to another as if talking were an unnecessary noise, as if you had already understood everything."

"I'm afraid she was more intelligent than I am."

"I didn't say that. Try again."

I tried. I got it. Jeanne gave me a cigarette, offered me a light, studied me: "You smoke like her. Except that you smoke. She would take two drags and then put out the cigarette. You must get it into your head that whatever she touched she dropped immediately. She wasn't interested in an idea for more than a few seconds, she changed her clothes three times a day, little boys didn't last her a week; one day she liked grapefruit juice, the next day it was vodka. Two drags, and out. It's not difficult. You can light another right away, that'll be good."

"That's expensive, isn't it?"

"That's you talking, not her. Never say that again."

She put me at the wheel of the Fiat. After a little practice I was able to drive it without too much risk.

"What became of the MG?"

"It burned with the rest. They found it crushed in the

garage. It's crazy, you hold the wheel the way she did. You weren't so dumb, you know how to observe. And then we must realize that you have never driven any car but hers. If you're good, I'll give you one as a reward when we're in the south. With 'your' money."

She dressed me like Micky, made me up like Micky. Full skirts of thick wool, petticoats, underwear in white, sea green, sky blue. Raffermi shoes.

"How was it, when you were a heel-maker?"

"Rotten. Turn a little so I can see."

"My head hurts when I turn."

"You have pretty legs. She did too, I think—I can't remember. She held her chin higher, like this, look. Walk."

I walked. I sat down. I got up. I did a waltz step. I opened a drawer. I extended a finger, Neapolitan style, while I talked. My laugh was sharper, more distinct. I stood straight, legs apart, one foot perpendicular to the other. I said, "Murneau, the craziest thing, *ciao,* it's mad, I assure you, poor me, I love, I don't love, you know, a bunch of creeps." I held my head quizzically, with a sidelong glance.

"Not bad. When you sit down in a skirt like that, don't show your legs too much. Put them side by side, parallel, like this. There are times when I can't remember what she used to do."

"Any better than I do, you mean."

"That's not what I said."

"It's what you're thinking. You're losing your nerve. I'm doing my best, you know. All this is driving me crazy."

"I'm sure it is. Go on."

It was Micky's poor revenge. More real than the Domenica I had been, it was she who drove my tired legs, my exhausted mind.

One day Jeanne drove me to see some of the dead girl's friends. She never left my side, she said how unhappy I was; everything went off well.

Starting the next day, I was allowed to answer the telephone. They were sorry for me, they were mad with worry, they begged me to talk to them for five minutes. Jeanne listened in and explained afterward who had spoken to me.

She was not there, however, the morning that Gabriel, the old Do's lover, called. He said he knew about my troubles and explained himself who he was.

"I want to see you," he added.

I could not remember how to disguise my voice. Anxiety about making a mistake reduced me to silence.

"Do you understand?" he said.

"I can't see you right now. I need to think. You don't know what a state I'm in."

"Listen to me: I must see you. I haven't been able to reach you for three months, I'm not going to let you go now. There are certain things I have to know. I'm coming over."

"I won't let you in."

"Then watch out," he said. "I have a nasty trait: I'm stubborn. I couldn't care less about your troubles. Do's are more serious: she's dead. Do I come or not?"

"Please, you don't understand. I don't want to see anyone. Give me a little time. I promise I'll see you later."

"I'm coming," he said.

Jeanne arrived before he did and received him. I heard

their voices in the downstairs hallway. I was lying on my bed with one gloved fist against my mouth. After a moment, the front door closed again and Jeanne came and took me in her arms.

"He's not dangerous. He probably thinks he'd be a heel if he didn't come and ask you how his little friend died, but it goes no further than that. Calm down."

"I don't want to see him."

"You won't see him. It's all over. He's gone."

I was invited out. I met people who did not know what to say to me, so they asked Jeanne questions and told me to keep my chin up.

Jeanne even arranged a little party at rue de Courcelles one rainy afternoon. It was two or three days before we left for Nice. A sort of acid test or dress rehearsal, before I was graduated to my new life.

I was separated from her in a room on the first floor when I saw Francois Roussin, who had not been invited, come in. She had seen him too and she worked her way calmly toward me from one group to another.

Francois explained to me that he was not there in the role of an insistent lover, but as a secretary accompanying his employer. Nevertheless he seemed very much inclined to let the lover talk when Jeanne succeeded in joining us.

"Leave her alone, or I'll throw you out," she told him.

"Never make threats you can't carry out. Listen, Murneau, so help me I'll knock you flat if you keep on bothering me."

They were talking in low voices, without even losing their friendly manner. I took Jeanne's arm and asked Francois to go away.

"I must talk to you, Micky," he insisted.

"We've already talked."

"There are things I haven't told you."

"You've told me enough."

I pulled Jeanne away from him. He left immediately. I saw him talking to Francois Chance, and as he was putting on his overcoat in the hallway, his glance met mine. There was nothing in his eyes but a kind of rage; I turned away.

In the evening, when everyone had left, Jeanne held me against her a long time, and told me that I had fulfilled her expectations, that we were going to succeed, that we had succeeded.

Nice.

Micky's father, Georges Isola, was very thin, very pale, very old. He looked at me, nodding his head, his eyes full of tears, not daring to kiss me. When he did, his sobs brought forth my own. I lived an absurd moment, for I was neither afraid nor unhappy, but overcome with joy to see him so happy. I believe that for a few minutes I forgot I was not Micky.

I promised to come and see him again. I assured him that I was well. I left him some presents and cigarettes with the feeling that it was hateful. Jeanne took me away. In the car she let me cry my fill, but then she apologized and said she would have to take advantage of my emotion: she had made an appointment with Dr. Chaveres. She drove me right to his office. She thought it would be better all around for him to see me in this state.

As a matter of fact he thought that the visit to my father had upset me to the point of endangering my recovery. He found me physically and mentally exhausted, and advised Jeanne to isolate me a while longer; just what she was hoping for.

He was as I remembered him: heavy, with close-cut hair and thick butcher's hands. Yet I had only seen him once, between two flashes of light, before or after my operation. He told me how worried his brother-in-law, Dr. Doulin, was, and showed me the report the latter had sent him.

"Why did you stop seeing him?"

"Those sessions," Jeanne interrupted, "upset her terribly. I called him. He decided himself that it was better to discontinue them."

Chaveres, who was older and perhaps more forceful than Dr. Doulin, told Jeanne that he was addressing me, and that he would be grateful if she would leave me alone with him. She refused.

"I want to know what happens to her. I trust you, but I won't leave her alone with anyone. You can speak in front of me."

"What do you know about it?" he said. "I see from these reports that you have been present at all her interviews with Dr. Doulin. He got nothing out of her after she left the clinic. Do you want to help her get well or don't you?"

"I want Jeanne to stay," I said. "If she has to go, I'll go too. Dr. Doulin promised me my memory would come back in a very short time. I did what he wanted. I played with blocks and had shock treatments. I told him my troubles for hours on end. He gave me injections. If he made a mistake, it's not Jeanne's fault."

"He made a mistake," sighed Chaveres, "but I'm beginning to understand why."

I saw my pages of automatic writing in the file he had opened.

"He made a mistake?" marveled Jeanne.

"Oh! Please don't say that as if you knew what it meant. This poor girl is not suffering from any injury. Her memories stop at the age of five or six, like those of a senile old man; the habits have persisted. Any specialist in the diseases of memory and speech would consider this a lacunary amnesia. The shock, the emotion . . . at her age it might last three weeks or three months. If Dr. Doulin made a mistake, he certainly realized that he did, otherwise I wouldn't know it. I'm a surgeon, not a psychiatrist. Have you read what she wrote?"

"I've read it."

"What's so peculiar about the words *hands, hair, eyes, nose, mouth?* These are words that recur all the time."

"I don't know."

"Neither do I, believe me. What I do know is that this girl was sick *before* the accident. Was she high-strung, violent, egocentric? Did she have a tendency to feel sorry for herself, to cry in her sleep, to have nightmares? Were you familiar with her sudden rages, like that day she tried to hit my brother-in-law with her hand still in a cast?"

"I don't understand. Micky is emotional, she is twenty years old, it's possible that she is somewhat violent by nature, but she was not sick. Actually, she was very sensible."

"Good God! I never said she wasn't sensible! Let's understand each other. Before the fire, this girl, like more people than there are pipe smokers or stamp collectors, presented certain characteristics of an hysterical nature. If I claim she was sick, it is first of all a personal opinion as to the point where illness begins. And also because certain amnesias or aphasias are among the traditional stigmata of hysteria."

He rose, walked round the desk, came over to where I was sitting next to Jeanne on a leather couch. He took me by the chin and turned my head toward Jeanne.

"Does she look senile? Her amnesia is not lacunary, but elective. So you may understand, I will simplify. She has not forgotten a definite slice of her life, a temporal slice, even the largest. She *refuses* to remember something or someone. Do you know how Dr. Doulin arrived at that? Because even as far back as the age of four or five, there are gaps. This something or someone must, directly or indirectly, touch so many memories since her birth that she has erased them all, one after another. Do you understand what I mean? Have you ever thrown stones into the water? Those eccentric figures that spread from circle to circle, it's like that."

He let go of my chin and drew circles in the air.

"If you look at my X rays and the report on the operation," he continued, "you will see that my role was limited to sewing her up. One hundred and forty stitches. Believe me, my hand was steady that night, and I'm in a position to know that I did not damage her. This is not a case of injury, not even the after-effect of a physical shock; her heart would tell us that better than her head. This is the characteristic psychic withdrawal of a child who was *already* sick."

I could endure it no longer. I got up, asked Jeanne to take me away. He held me back forcibly by the arm.

"I want to frighten you," he said, raising his voice.

"Left to yourself you may recover, you may not. But if I have one word of advice, one truth, one good to give you, it is to come and see me again. And also to think about this: this fire was not your fault, this girl did not die because of you. Whether or not you refuse to remember her, she did exist. She was pretty, she was your age, her name was Domenica Loi, she is really dead, and there's nothing you can do about it."

He caught my arm before I could hit him. He told Jeanne he was counting on her to see that I came again.

We stayed in Nice three days, in a hotel facing the sea. The month of October was ending but there were still bathers on the beach. As I watched them from the window of our room, I persuaded myself that I recognized this town, this taste of salt and seaweed in the air.

Jeanne would not have taken me back to Dr. Chaveres for anything in the world. She considered him an idiot of the rude variety. He was not hysterical, but paranoid. From sewing up other people's heads, his brain had turned into a pincushion. He was the one with holes in his head.

I, however, would have liked to have seen him again. He was rude, to be sure, but I was sorry I had interrupted him. He had not told me everything.

"He imagines that you want to forget yourself!" said Jeanne ironically. "That's what it boils down to."

"If he knew who I am he'd change his story, don't be silly. I want to forget Micky, that's all."

"On the contrary, if he changed his story, his perfect argument wouldn't hold for a minute. I don't know what he means by hysteria; I could almost admit that at times Micky needed treatment, but you were perfectly normal. I've never seen you high-strung or impossible the way she used to be."

"I'm the one who tried to hit Dr. Doulin, I'm the one who hit you. You can't deny that!"

"In your place and the state you were in, I imagine anyone would have done the same. I would have used a sledge hammer. Which does not negate the fact that you also took a beating that left you bruised for a week without even daring to defend yourself, from a crazy girl who couldn't have weighed an ounce more than you. But it's you we're talking about, not her!"

On the third day she announced that we were going back to Cap Cadet. It was almost time for the opening of the will. She had to be present, and she would have to leave me alone with a servant for a few days. She still did not consider me equal to playing my role in Florence. At Cap Cadet, where repairs had started two weeks after the fire, only Domenica's room was still uninhabitable. There I would be away from people, and I would undoubtedly find an atmosphere which would facilitate my recovery.

On this subject we had our first quarrel since the day I had run away from her on the street in Paris. The idea of returning to the villa, where all traces of the fire could not have been obliterated, even the idea of getting well there, terrified me. As always, I gave in.

In the afternoon Jeanne left me alone for an hour on the terrace of the hotel. She returned in a different car from her own, a sky blue Fiat 1500 *cabriolet,* and told me that it was mine. She gave me the keys and the registration, and I took her for a drive in Nice.

The next morning we took the Corniche and the Toulon road, she in front in her car, I behind in mine.

We arrived at Cap Cadet in the afternoon. Mme. Yvette was waiting for us, doggedly sweeping up the plaster and debris left by the workmen. She was afraid to tell me that she did not recognize me, but burst into tears and retreated to the kitchen, repeating with a pronounced southern accent, "Poor girl, poor girl."

The house was low with an almost flat roof. The outside painting had not been finished. Large soot marks remained on the side the fire had spared. They had repaired the garage and the dining room where Mme. Yvette served us in the evening.

"I don't know whether you still like mullet," she told me, "but I thought you might enjoy it. How does it feel to be back?"

"Leave her alone," interrupted Jeanne.

I tasted the fish and pronounced it very good. Mme. Yvette was somewhat consoled at this.

"You might be a little more human, you know, Murneau," she said to Jeanne. "I'm not going to eat her."

When she brought the fruit she leaned down and kissed me on the cheek. She said that Murneau was not the only one who had worried about me. Not a day had gone by the last three months without someone in Les Lecques asking her for news.

"There's even a *niston,* he came again yesterday afternoon while I was cleaning the upstairs. You must have been nice to him!"

"A what?"

"A *niston,* a kid. He can't be much older than you. Twenty-two, twenty-three, maybe. Nothing to be ashamed of either. Looks like a Greek god, he does, and smells as good as you do. I know because I gave him a smooch, I've known him since he was knee-high."

"And Micky knew him?" asked Jeanne.

"Must have. He never stops asking me when you're coming back and where you are."

Jeanne was looking at her with an air of annoyance.

"Oh, he'll come all right," concluded Mme. Yvette. "He's not far away. He works at the post office in La Ciotat."

At one o'clock in the morning, lying in bed in the room Micky had occupied at the beginning of the summer, I was still awake. Mme. Yvette had gone back to Les Lecques. A little before midnight I had heard Jeanne walk into my old room and go into the rebuilt bathroom. She was probably making sure no awkward indication remained in spite of the investigation and the workmen.

Then she had gone to bed in the third room at the end of the hall. I got up and went in to her. I found her lying on her unmade bed in a white slip, reading a book entitled *Maladies of the Memory* by someone named Delay.

"Don't walk barefoot," she told me. "Sit down or else put on my shoes. I must have some slippers in my bags somewhere."

I put the book I had taken from her hands on a table and dropped down beside her.

"Who is this boy, Jeanne?"

"I know nothing about him."

"Exactly what did I say on the telephone?"

"Nothing that should keep you awake. To be dangerous, he'd have to have had access to both the telegram and our calls. That is hardly likely."

"Is the post office in La Ciotat big?"

"I don't know. We'll have to make a trip there tomorrow. Now go back to bed. Anyway, I'm not sure telephone calls go through La Ciotat."

"There's a telephone here. I saw one downstairs. We could find out right now."

"Don't be a fool. Go back to bed."

"Can I sleep with you?"

In the darkness she suddenly said that there was another snag much more upsetting than this.

"I found a monkey wrench in the bathroom with a pile of half-burned stuff. It was in the bottom of a wash pail. It's not mine. The one I used that night I threw away. It's possible that you bought one somewhere, when you were unscrewing the nut every day."

"I would have told you so. I would have got rid of it."

"I don't know, I hadn't thought of that. I thought you took the one in the tool kit in the MG. In any case, the investigators didn't see it, or if they did, they didn't think it was important."

Later I leaned over to see whether she was asleep. I asked her in the dark why she had stayed with me since that first afternoon at the clinic—if it was only because of the will after all, to play the game. As she did not answer, I told her that I wanted with all my heart to regain my memory and help her. I told her that I loved my sky blue car and everything she had given me.

She answered that she was asleep.

In the days that followed, I continued what Jeanne called my "training." I could observe my progress by watching Mme. Yvette's reactions. Several times a day she would say, "Ah, you haven't changed!"

I forced myself to be livelier, more exuberant, because at times Jeanne accused me of being listless, saying, "That's perfect, just keep that up and we'll be walking the streets of South America together. French prisons aren't much fun."

Since Mme. Yvette was at the villa almost all day, we were forced to go out. Jeanne would take me to Bandol, as Micky must have done three months before, or else we would lie on the sunniest part of the beach. One afternoon a fisherman going by in his boat seemed surprised to see a fall tourist in a bathing suit and white gloves.

The boy Mme. Yvette had spoken of had not come. The La Ciotat post office looked large enough so that we dismissed the idea of an indiscretion, but telephone calls to Cap Cadet were indeed routed through it.

Four days before the opening of the will Jeanne put a bag in the back of her car and left. The night before, we had gone to Marseille in my car for dinner. At the table she had talked to me unexpectedly—about her parents (she was born in Caserte, an Italian in spite of her name), her beginnings with La Raffermi, the "good period" she had enjoyed between eighteen and twenty-six—in a calm, pleasant voice. On the way back, while I was driving around all the curves between Cassis and La Ciotat, she had let her head slip onto my shoulder and put her arm around me, helping me hold the wheel whenever I swerved.

She had promised not to stay in Florence any longer than necessary to clear up certain aspects of the will. The week before her death La Raffermi had added to the will in a second envelope a clause setting the date of its opening at my coming of age, in the event she died before that time. It was either an old woman's childish prank, to annoy Micky (Jeanne's theory), or simply because she felt herself declining rapidly and wanted to effect a delay so her businessmen could bring her accounts up to date (Francois Chance's theory). I did not understand how this changed matters, but Jeanne said that a codicil could create more problems than the pure and simple replacement of a will, and that in any case several of Raffermi's intimates would take advantage of this or some other irregularity to make trouble for us.

It had been agreed since our visit to Micky's father that Jeanne would pick him up on her way through Nice. As she said good-by to me, Mme. Yvette's presence prevented her from giving me any instructions except to go to bed early and be good.

Mme. Yvette moved into Jeanne's room. That first night I could not sleep. I went down to the kitchen for a glass of water. Then, since it looked like a beautiful night, I put on a jacket of Jeanne's over my nightgown and went out. In the dark I walked around the villa. Slipping my hands into the pockets of the jacket, I found a pack of cigarettes. I leaned back against a wall in the corner of the garage and put one in my mouth.

Someone beside me held out a match.

I MURDER

THE BOY APPEARED in the June sun just after Micky had closed her magazine. She was lying on the little pebbled beach at the foot of the promontory. At first he seemed enormous to her because he was standing over her in a white shirt and faded canvas pants, but later she saw that he was of medium height, even rather short. He was very attractive though, with big black eyes, a straight nose, a girl's mouth, and a curious way of standing stiffly with his shoulders hunched and his hands in his pockets.

For two or three weeks now, Micky and Do had been living in the villa at Cap Cadet. Micky was alone this afternoon because Do had taken the car to go and buy something or other in a shop in La Ciotat: a pair of slacks they had looked at together and which she found hideous, or some pink earrings, equally hideous. At any rate, that is what Micky told the boy later.

He came quietly, without moving the pebbles under his feet. He was slender, and he had the watchful quickness of a cat.

Micky put her sunglasses back on to get a better look at him. She sat up, holding up the unfastened top of her bikini with one hand. He asked her, without an accent, whether she was Micky. Then without waiting for the answer, he sat down beside her, not quite facing her, with a wonderfully fluid movement, as if this were all he did in life. She told him for form's sake that it was a private beach and she would be grateful if he went away.

As she seemed to be having some trouble fastening her bathing suit top behind her back, he leaned over quickly and before she realized it he had done it himself.

After that he said he was going for a swim. He took off his shirt, his pants, and his espadrilles, and clad in an old pair of khaki shorts, he walked off toward the water.

He swam the way he walked, calmly, silently. He came back with short locks of brown hair on his forehead, and searched his pants pockets for cigarettes. He offered Micky a Gauloise which had lost almost half of its tobacco. A drop of water fell on the girl's thigh as he gave her a light.

"Do you know why I'm here?"

Micky replied that it was not hard to guess.

"I'd be surprised," he said. "Oh, I have all the girls I want. I've been watching you for a week, but believe me, it's not for that. Anyway, it's your friend I'm watching. She's not bad either, but what I'm interested in doesn't show. It's here."

He placed a finger on his forehead, fell back and stretched out in the sun, his cigarette in his mouth and one arm under his head. After a full minute of silence he turned his eyes, took his Gauloise out of his mouth, and declared, "My God, you're not curious?"

"What do you want?"

"Well, it's about time. What do you think I want? Ten thousand? Five hundred thousand? What's it worth to keep your little heart beating? The movie stars are insured. Arms, legs, the whole works. Are you insured?"

Micky seemed to relax. She took off her glasses so she would not be white around the eyes, and said she had already had this routine. He could keep his shirt on, literally.

"Don't get me wrong," he said. "I'm not selling insurance."

"I know that."

"I'm just a good guy. I know how to keep my eyes and ears open, and I want you to take advantage of some information. Besides, I don't make much money. For a hundred thousand I'll spill the beans."

"If I'd given in every time someone's put the touch on me, I'd be through. Are you going to put your clothes on or not?"

He sat up as if he'd given up his strange ideas. Without moving his hips, just by lifting his legs a little, he put on his pants. Micky found him fascinating to watch. Later she told him so. At the time she merely observed him through half-shut eyes.

"First of all, Jeanne's out of her mind. Do you know what her sign is? Taurus. Look out for Taurus, sweetie,

*they've got the hide of an elephant. Everything in the
head and nothing in the heart . . ."*

Micky put her sunglasses back on. He looked at her,
smiled, put on his shirt and espadrilles and got up. She
held him back by the bottom of his pant leg.

"Where did you hear that?"

"A hundred."

"You heard me say it, in a restaurant in Bandol. You
heard us talking, didn't you?"

"I haven't been to Bandol since last summer. I work
in La Ciotat, in the post office. I get off at four-thirty.
I heard that today, less than an hour ago. I was about
to leave. Have you made up your mind, yes or no?"

Micky got to her knees and probably to gain time,
asked him for another cigarette. He lit it himself and
handed it to her as he had undoubtedly seen it done
in the movies.

"At the post office? Was it a phone call?"

"Florence," he said. "I'm a good guy. I guarantee you,
it's easily worth a hundred! All I need is money, like
everybody else. It's nothing to you."

"You're ridiculous, go away."

"Your friend was the one that made the call," he
said. "The one on the other end talks like this: 'Think
it over. That will do. Hang up.' "

Just then Micky heard the MG pull up in front of
the villa: Do coming back. She lowered her dark glasses,
looked the boy up and down one more time, and told
him all right, he would have the money if the information was worth it.

"I'll talk when I see the hundred," he said. "Be at
the *tabac* in Les Lecques tonight at midnight. There's
an outdoor movie in the courtyard. I'll be there."

He left without another word. Micky waited for Do to come and find her. When the girl arrived in her bathing suit with a towel over her shoulders, looking relaxed and happy, Micky told herself that she would not go to the *tabac* tonight or ever. It was late and the sun was getting low.

"What did you do?"

"Nothing," said Do. "Just loafed. How's the water?"

She was wearing the pink earrings. She went into the water the way she always did, first carefully wetting herself all over, then jumping in with a loud war whoop.

On the way to Bandol for dinner that evening, Micky glanced at the *tabac* in Les Lecques as they went by. In the courtyard behind the building she saw lights and movie posters.

"I met a strange boy this afternoon," she told Do. "A strange boy with strange ideas."

And since Do did not respond, she added that she was going to have fun in this place after all.

At twenty minutes to twelve she took Do back to the villa, said she had forgotten to stop at the drugstore, that one would be open in La Ciotat. She turned the headlights back on and left.

At ten minutes to twelve she left the car in a little side street near the Les Lecques *bar-tabac* and went into a canvas-covered courtyard. Sitting on a folding chair, she saw the end of a cloak-and-dagger movie without being able to locate her little crook among the other spectators.

When she came out he was waiting for her, standing in front of the counter of the *bar-tabac* with his eyes glued to the television set, the sleeves of a navy blue sweater knotted around his neck.

"Let's sit down," he said, bringing his glass.

In an empty terrace, behind glass partitions which the headlights constantly splashed with light, Micky took from the pocket of her cardigan two ten-thousand-franc bills and one five-thousand-franc bill.

"If what you have to tell me is so interesting, you'll get the rest."

"I'm a good guy. I trust you. And then, I know that right now you want to get home."

He took the bills, folded them carefully, and put them in his pocket. He said that a few days ago he had transmitted a telegram from Florence. Since the errand boy was out for the morning, he had had to deliver it himself.

"Café de la Desirade, in La Ciotat."

"What does this have to do with me?" said Micky.

"It was addressed to you."

"I don't receive my mail in cafés."

"Your friend does. It was she who came for it. I know, because she stopped at the post office a few minutes later. I admit that at the time I still thought nothing of it. I got interested when she wanted to call Florence. The girl who put the call through is a pal of mine. I listened in. I found out it was the one who sent the telegram."

"Who, in Florence?"

"I don't know. The telegram wasn't signed. It's a girl who answers the phone. She sounds like somebody who knows what she wants. Unless I miss my guess, she's the one you get in touch with when you need money. Know who it is?"

Micky nodded her head, a little pale.

"What did the telegram say?"

"That's the hard part," said the boy, making a face. "I think someone's impersonating you for the dough, something like that, but if it's more serious I have to be covered. What if I make a mistake and you have to go to the cops? What would happen to me? I don't want anyone to think this is blackmail."

"There's no question of my going to the police."

"That's what I thought. Too much talk. Anyway, all I want is to be covered."

"Whatever happens, I promise I won't talk about you. Is that what you want?"

"Very funny," said the boy. "I don't know anything about you and I care less. The same goes for your promises. The receipt for the telegram is my only guarantee. Sign the book, and we're in business."

He explained that there was a record of the receipt of telegrams. As a rule the delivery boy did not bother to ask for a signature. He only made a note of the date and put an X in the blank space.

"You sign in the space for your telegram as if you had received it yourself at the Café de la Desirade, and if you double-cross me, I can still defend myself."

Micky replied that he could not be serious, that she was already bored with the whole business. He could consider himself lucky to have made twenty-five thousand francs out of such drivel. She was sleepy, she would leave him to his pleasures.

She got up and left the terrace. He caught up with her in front of the MG in the dark little street. He gave her back the bills, leaned over and kissed her lightly on the mouth, opened the car door, took from the seat a big black notebook that had somehow gotten there, whispered, "Clarissa coupling. Fondly," and was gone.

She met him again on the road outside of Les Lecques, standing calmly on an embankment waiting for a ride. Micky found him a little too clever. However, she parked her car a little farther on and waited for him to get in. With his stiff shoulders, his fluid movements, and his lowered eyes, he still looked like a bad boy, but he could not conceal his satisfaction.

"Do you have something to write with?"

He handed her a pencil and opened the black notebook.

"Where do I sign?"

"Here."

He examined the signature carefully by the light of the dashboard, leaning so close that she smelled his hair and asked him what he put on it.

"A man's cologne, a brand you can only get in Algeria. I served in the army down there."

"It's quite repulsive. Move away, and tell me again what that telegram says."

He repeated: "Clarissa coupling. Fondly." Then he repeated three times all he remembered of the first telephone call. He had listened to another one that day, just before he decided to come to the beach and speak to her. He had been hanging around the outskirts of the villa for the past week from five o'clock in the afternoon until dinner time.

Micky said nothing. Eventually he fell silent too. After reflecting for a long minute with knitted brows, she put the car into first and started off again. She drove him to the port of La Ciotat, where the cafés were still open,

and a big boat was sleeping surrounded by little ones.
Before he got out, he asked her whether she was worried
about what he had told her.

"I don't know yet."

"Do you want me to find out what's going on?"

"Go away and forget about it."

"Okay."

He got out of the car, but before closing the door he
leaned over and held out his hand.

"I'll forget about it, but first . . ."

She gave him the twenty-five thousand francs.

At two o'clock in the morning when she went up to
the second floor, Domenica was asleep. Micky entered
the first bathroom by the hall door. The name "Clarissa"
reminded her of something, she did not know what,
and it was connected with the bathroom. She turned
on the light and saw the trademark on the water heater.
Her eyes followed the gas pipe up to the top of the
walls.

"Anything the matter?" asked Domenica, stirring in
her bed in the next room.

"Need your toothpaste."

Micky put out the light, went out through the hall,
and went to bed.

A little before noon the next day, Micky told Mme.
Yvette that she and Do would have lunch in Cassis.
She apologized for forgetting to tell her about it and
gave her an errand to do in the afternoon.

Stopping the MG in front of the post office in La
Ciotat, she told Do, "Come on, there's something I've

been meaning to send for days now. It's always slipping my mind."

They went inside. Micky studied her friend's face out of the corner of her eye: Do was visibly ill at ease. As bad luck would have it, an employee asked pleasantly, "Is it for Florence?"

Micky pretended not to have heard, took a telegram form from a counter, and wrote out a message to Jeanne Murneau. She had given it a lot of thought before going to sleep, and had planned every word:

"Forgive me, desperate, money, I kiss you a thousand times everywhere: forehead, eyes, nose, mouth, hands, feet, be nice, I'm crying, your Mi." If Jeanne found the words strange and was worried, the plan would be stopped. She would have had her chance.

Micky showed the message to Do, who read it without finding it either particularly amusing or particularly strange.

"I think it's quite funny," said Micky. "Just what the doctor ordered. Will you take it to the window? I'll wait for you in the car."

The boy from the night before, still in a white shirt, was stamping papers behind a window. He had seen them come into the post office and was standing near by. He followed Micky out.

"What are you going to do?"

"Nothing," said Micky. "If you want the rest of the money, you're the one who's going to do it. When you leave at five, go right to the villa. The housekeeper will be out. Go up to the second floor, first door on the right. It's a bathroom. After that you're on your own. You'll need a monkey wrench."

"What do they have against you?" he said.

"I don't know anything about it. If I've understood, you will too. Report tonight at the *tabac*. Around ten, if that's convenient for you."

"What will you have with you?"

"I can give you twenty-five thousand francs more. After that, you may have to wait a few days."

"Look, so far for me this is strictly girl stuff. If it turns out to be anything more serious, count me out."

"As soon as I know what's going on it won't be serious," said Micky. "Besides, you're right: it's strictly girl stuff."

He waited for her that night in the little street where she had parked the night before.

"Don't get out," he said, "we're getting out of here. I don't want to be seen twice with you in the same place."

They drove along the Les Lecques beach, then Micky took the road to Bandol.

"I'm not getting mixed up in anything like this," he said. "Not even for ten times the money."

"I need you."

"All you have to do is get the cops pronto. You won't have to draw them a picture. All they have to do is unscrew the pipe and read the telegram: those two are out to get you."

"It's more complicated than that," said Micky. "I can't go for the police. I need you to stop this, but I'll need Domenica even more, and for years. Don't try to understand, I don't feel like explaining."

"The one in Florence, who is she?"

"Her name is Jeanne."

"Does she want your money that bad?"

"Actually, I don't think she does. Anyway that's not the real reason, but that doesn't concern anyone: the police, or you, or Domenica."

She was silent until they reached Bandol. They drove to the Casino at the end of the beach, but they did not get out when she turned off the motor.

"Do you understand how they're going to do it?" asked Micky, turning to the boy.

That night she was wearing turquoise pants, sandals, and the cardigan of the night before. She had taken out the ignition key and several times as she talked she pressed it against her cheek.

"I spent ten minutes in that bathroom," said the boy. "I saw that 'Clarissa' was the trademark on the water heater. I unscrewed the coupling nut over the window. That cardboard thing is all damp and soggy. There are other couplings in the hall, but I didn't bother to look at them. One is enough for their purposes. All they need is a closed room and the pilot of the water heater. Who took care of the installation? It's new."

"A plumber in La Ciotat."

"But who was there when the work was being done?"

"Jeanne must have come down in February or March. She's the one who took care of that."

"Then she may have an identical nut. This is a special kind of nut. Even if that filter thing was shot, it wouldn't let the gas escape fast enough to cause an explosion. And if they broke a nut, it would show. They must have another one."

"Are you willing to help me?"

"What's in it for me?"

"What you asked for: ten times as much."

"First I'd really like to know what's going on inside

your head," he said, after a moment's thought. "The imitation bit over the phone is confusing, but it makes sense. I've watched that girl better than anyone ever will, for hours at a time. She's sure to go through with it."

"I don't think so," said Micky.

"What are you planning to do?"

"Nothing, I told you. I need you to keep watching her. Jeanne will soon be here. What I would like to know is, when they plan to set fire to the house."

"They may not have decided yet."

"When they do decide, I want to know about it. If I do, I guarantee nothing will happen, nothing at all."

"Good. I'll try. Is that all?"

"Most evenings there's no one in the villa for hours at a time. Could you check the condition of the cardboard thing after we've left? Maybe that will tell us something. I won't be able to keep her from going ahead with it. All she has to do is close the door when she takes a bath."

"Why don't you confront them with it point-blank?" asked the boy. "Do you know what you're playing with right now?"

"Fire," said Micky. Laughing briefly, joylessly, she started the motor.

On the way back she talked mostly about him, about the way he moved, which she liked. He was thinking that she was pretty, the most attractive girl he had met, but that he ought to be sensible. Even if she agreed on the spot to go somewhere with him and let him make love to her, ten times a hundred thousand francs would last longer than the moment they would spend together.

As if she could read his mind, she took one hand off the wheel and gave him the money she had promised for the evening.

Anyway he lived with his parents, and it was always a pain in the neck finding a place.

He did what she asked. Four times in one week he saw the girls go off in the MG to spend the evening God knew where. He got into the villa through the garage which was always open, and examined the filter plate.

He ran into the little heiress with the long black hair twice: one afternoon when she was alone on the beach at the foot of the promontory, and one evening at a restaurant in the port of La Ciotat. She seemed relaxed, as if she were sure she had the situation in hand. She maintained that nothing was going to happen.

Her attitude changed abruptly after the arrival of the tall girl with the golden hair.

He watched all three of them for another whole week before Micky got in touch with him. Usually he stayed on the edge of the road behind the house, but sometimes he came near and listened to their voices in the rooms. One afternoon Micky came back alone from the little beach, barefoot, in a bathing suit. She made an appointment with him for that evening.

They met at the port in La Ciotat. She did not get out of the MG. She gave him five ten-thousand-franc bills and announced that she no longer required his services. For his information, the tall girl had noticed him several times near the house. Anyway, the plan was only a joke, she knew that now. She advised him good-naturedly to be happy with the money he had received and to forget the whole thing. If he bothered her in any way at all, she was determined to make it unpleasant for him and she had ways of doing so.

Before leaving, the MG went ten yards, stopped, and backed up again until it came opposite the boy. Micky leaned over the door and said, "By the way, I don't even know your name."

He replied that there was no reason why she should.

I HAD MURDERED

HE SAID his name was Serge Reppo. At first, when I had tried to scream, he had clapped his hand over my mouth and pushed me inside the garage. When he realized that I no longer meant to scream, that I was listening to him, he had been content to hold me against him, trapped between my car and the wall, with my right arm twisted behind my back. He had talked at least half an hour without releasing me in a low, anxious voice, tightening his grip on me whenever I struggled. I was bent over backward on the front of the Fiat; my legs were numb.

The sliding door of the garage had been left half open. The moon outlined a large patch of light at its base. The boy's face, near my own, seemed, when it shifted, to shift the edge of the darkness as well.

"After that," he said, "I forgot about it. On the fifth of July I heard that the fire had actually killed someone, and that changed everything. At first I thought that Domenica had been the smartest, then I asked myself a few questions. I combed the newspapers, I pumped the local people, but I didn't find out anything. What bothered me was the amnesia."

As he had been doing more and more often in the last few minutes, he took a deep breath and secured his hold on me by pushing me back farther against the car. He must have been a little older than Mme. Yvette had said, or else it was the little wrinkles at the corners of the eyes that aged him when his face moved into the moonlight.

I was out of breath. I still wanted to scream, but I would not have been able.

"Three months," he said. "I swear I turned over a new leaf. And then you came back. When I saw you with the tall blonde, I realized that the other one hadn't made it, that you were Micky. Of course I had my doubts; you've changed a little since July. This hair, this face, don't tell me they're you! But I've watched you the last few days. All that coaching, walk like this, button your jacket like that, is a lot of crap . . . Frankly, I didn't think there was much in it for me. But now I don't have many scruples left. I'm the one who tipped you off; well, I want my cut, get it?"

I shook my head in despair, and he misunderstood my meaning.

"Don't be a fool!" he said, pulling me suddenly against him, my back throbbing. "I believe you were hit on the head; if that were a crock, you could tell. But you know very well you killed her!"

This time I nodded my head.

"Let me go, please."

It was only a whisper, he must have read my lips rather than heard it.

"But you understand?"

I nodded my head again, exhausted. He hesitated, released my wrist, and drew back a little, but kept one hand on my hip as if he were still afraid I was capable of escaping. It was this hand that kept me from falling backward against the hood of the car. I felt his perspiration through my nightgown.

"When does your friend get back?"

"I don't know. In a few days. Please let me go. I won't scream. I won't run away."

I pushed his hand away. He moved back against the garage wall and we remained silent for a long moment. I leaned against my car to hold myself up. The garage went around once, twice, but I stayed upright. I realized then that my feet were like ice, that I had lost my slippers when he had pushed me into the garage. I asked him to get them for me.

He gave them to me, and when I had managed to put them back on, he took a step toward me again.

"I didn't mean to scare you. On the contrary, I've got good reason to want to be friends. You're the one who forced me to be rough. Actually it's very simple: I can bother you or leave you alone. I don't want to bother you. You promised me one million francs; you'll give me two, one for you, one for the tall blonde. That's fair, isn't it?"

I said yes to everything. I longed only to be alone, away from him, to put my thoughts back in order. I would have promised him anything at all. He must

this, for he declared, "Just remember one
I have your signature on the register. I'll go
but I'm here, and I won't let you out of my
on't try anything. You made a fool of me
with me once is enough. I learn fast."

He moved back farther until he was completely visible
in the moonlight coming through the doorway.

"Can I count on you?"

I answered yes, yes, go away. Saying that he would see
me again, he disappeared. I did not hear him walk away
from the house. When I came out of the garage a moment later, the moon shone on an empty world. It was
almost as if I had just had another nightmare.

I did not close my eyes until daylight. The nape of
my neck and my back hurt again. I trembled under the
covers.

I tried to remember what he had said to me word
for word. But even in the garage, in spite of the position
he kept me in, every word he breathed in my face had
called up images. I had superimposed my own imagination on his account; everything was distorted.

Besides, whom was I to believe? I had never had a
life. I lived other people's dreams. Jeanne told me about
Micky in her own way, and that was a dream. I listened
to her in my own way, and when I told myself the same
story afterward, that too was a dream, a little further
from the truth.

Jeanne, Francois Roussin, Serge Reppo. Dr. Doulin,
Mme. Yvette: mirrors within mirrors. Nothing of what
I believed had really existed outside of my mind.

That night I did not even try to find an explanation
for the strange attitude of Serge Reppo's Micky, still

154

less to reconstruct once again that other night when the house had burned.

Endlessly, until dawn, I turned over in my mind meaningless details, like a donkey going around a well. For example, I pictured how Serge had moved when he leaned inside the MG to get the black notebook (why black? He had not said so). Had he kissed Micky (*I even gave you a casual peck*) on the cheek or on the mouth, leaning over or standing up? What if what he was telling me were true?

Or again, I recognized on myself the disgusting smell of that cheap cologne he doused his hair with. Micky had noticed it too. *Your signature, he had said, was very good, I checked right away by the light of the dashboard. You even asked me what I put on my hair. It's some special stuff that comes from Algeria, I was in the army down there. You see, I wouldn't make that up!*

Maybe he had told Micky the name of that cologne. But in the garage he had not told me—it had no name. More than the thought of the harm he could do us, Jeanne and me, that smell which I recognized or thought I recognized on my gloves and arms upset me so much that I had to turn my light on again. The blackmailer must be prowling around the house, around me. He was guarding me like his property: a mind, a memory that belonged to him.

I went to the bathroom and washed my face, and back to bed without breaking his spell. I did not know where to find sleeping pills. By the time I fell asleep the sunlight was already coming through my shutters.

Toward noon when Mme. Yvette, worried, woke me, it seemed to me that the smell was still on me. My first thought was that he would surely suspect that I would try to warn Jeanne. If I did, he would find out about it one way or another. He would become alarmed and go to the police. I must not do that.

After lunch I went out in front of the house. I did not see him. I believe I would have asked his permission to call Florence. I spent the next two days endlessly going over the most senseless plans for getting rid of him without warning Jeanne. I wandered aimlessly from the little beach to a couch on the first floor. He did not return.

The third day, which was my birthday, a cake Mme. Yvette had made for me reminded me of the opening of the will. Jeanne was going to telephone.

She called in the afternoon. Serge must have been at the post office. He would listen, he would realize that I was Do. I did not know how to ask Jeanne to come back. I said I was fine, that I longed to see her. She said she longed to see me too.

I was slow to perceive a strangeness in her voice because I was completely preoccupied with the presence I felt on our line, but eventually I did notice it.

"It's nothing," she said, "I'm tired. I'm having some problems here. I'll have to be away another day or two."

She told me not to worry, that she would explain when she got back. As we hung up, it was as if I were being cut off from her forever. But all I did was mechanically make a kissing sound into the receiver and say nothing.

A new morning, new fears.

As I looked out my bedroom window, two men were taking notes in front of the garage. They looked up and greeted me with nods. They looked like policemen.

When I came down they had gone. Mme. Yvette told me that they were employees of the La Ciotat fire department. They had come to check something, she did not know what: something to do with timbers and the north wind.

I thought, "they" are making a new investigation.

I went back up to my room to get dressed. I did not know what was going on. I trembled, I saw my hands tremble. I could not put my stockings on by myself, as I had finally learned to do. However, my mind was curiously immobile, paralyzed.

At one point, after standing barefoot for a long time in the middle of the room with my stockings in my hand, I heard a voice inside me say, "If Micky knew, she would have defended herself. She was stronger than you, you were alone, she would not be dead. This boy is lying." Another voice said, "Serge Reppo has already gone to the police. Those men did not come three months after the fire for the pleasure of annoying you. Run away, go to Jeanne."

I went out into the hall, half dressed. My steps led me like a sleepwalker to the burned room of Domenica.

A stranger was there, sitting on a window sill in a putty-colored raincoat. I must have heard him moving around and thought it was Serge, but it was a young man I had never seen before, thin, with sad eyes. He was not surprised at my entrance, or the way I was dressed, or my fright. I stood with my back against the door, the stockings I had in my hands against my mouth. We looked at each other for a long time without saying a word.

Now everything was empty, abandoned, burned: the

room without furniture with its ruined floor; my heart, which had stopped beating. I saw in his eyes that he despised me, that he was my enemy, that he too knew how to lead me to my destruction.

A half-burned shutter banged behind him. He rose and came slowly to the center of the room. He spoke. He had already spoken to me one day on the telephone. He was Gabriel, Domenica's lover. He said that I had murdered Domenica. He had had a premonition about it from the first day. Now he was sure, tomorrow he would have proof. He was a madman with a calm voice.

"What are you doing here?"

"I'm looking," he said. "I'm looking for you."

"You have no right to enter my house."

"You're the one who's going to give me the right."

He had waited, he was not in a hurry. He had been right to wait. As of the day before, he knew why I had killed Domenica. He even had a professional excuse to enter my house. All his expenses were being paid to spend as much time here as he needed to prove the murder.

The excuse was a life and retirement insurance policy taken out by the employees of the bank where Domenica had worked. It was through this insurance policy that they had met. He asked me whether I did not find life strange: he had waited three months, knowing that one clause in this policy would enable him to make his investigation. He had even made the last monthly payments out of his own pocket after he had learned of Do's death. If his company should discover this piece of dishonesty he would never find another job anywhere in his field; but in the meantime, he would have avenged his mistress.

I calmed down a little: he was trying to impress me, to show me how persistent he was, but he knew nothing.

He explained that in Italy things would be different. They would welcome him with open arms. In France Do had an insurance policy of only two thousand francs a month for ten years, but the various insurance policies taken out by Sandra Raffermi represented millions. If any objection at all operated with regard to an insignificant policy, the Italian insurance people would be more than keenly interested.

An objection? Raffermi's insurance? I did not understand. Again I was seized with anxiety. He even seemed a little surprised, then he must have guessed that I had not been informed of certain facts. This was the only time his face cleared, more with irony than good spirits.

"Tonight, tomorrow, if you prevent me from doing my job, this house will be full of worse snoopers than me," he said. "All I have to do is complain in my report of lack of cooperation on the part of a girl who has something to hide. I'm going to make another little tour of the house. I advise you to get dressed; we'll talk afterward."

He turned on his heel and walked calmly toward the burned bathroom. On the threshold he turned around. He said in a slow voice that my friend was having serious difficulties in Florence: *It was Do who had inherited the property*.

All afternoon I called Florence, numbers I had found in Jeanne's papers. Toward evening someone answered. They did not know where to get hold of Jeanne, but confirmed the fact that ten days before her last stroke, Raffermi had purely and simply drawn up a new will. I knew no Italian aside from expressions I had learned during the past few weeks, and Mme. Yvette, who was listening in, was not a very experienced interpreter. The conversation was barely comprehensible and I tried to convince myself that we had misunderstood.

Domenica's friend was walking around the house. He had not eaten lunch, he had not even taken off his raincoat. Sometimes he came over to me and, in spite of Mme. Yvette's presence, asked me questions like a detective, questions I could not answer.

He kept on. I did not dare send him away for fear of seeming even more suspicious to the others. I felt as if I were caught in the whirlpool of his steps.

He was there, walking in front of the house, when suddenly the whirlpool stopped at a single, mad idea: *Micky had a motive too—the same one I had! To take my place in order to recover her inheritance!*

I went up to my room. I took a coat and the money Jeanne had left me. I changed my gloves. When I opened the drawer where the clean ones were, I saw the little pearl-handled revolver we had found in one of Micky's bags. I hesitated a long time. Finally I took it.

Below, in front of the garage, the man in the raincoat watched me start my car without a word. As I was driving off, he called me back. He leaned over the car door and asked me whether I did not find life strange now: a pretty car was going to be my downfall.

"You knew that Do was going to inherit the money," he said. "You knew it because your aunt had told you so. You called her from Paris when your governess came to get you. It's written in black and white in the will. You celebrated Do's birthday, when you got home you drugged her with sleeping pills, shut her in her room, and set fire to the bathroom."

"You're completely mad!"

"You had foreseen everything, except for two things: first, that you would lose your memory with the rest and even forget your plan to impersonate Domenica; second, that the fire would not spread to the bedroom. Because it didn't!"

"I won't listen to another word. Go away!"

"Do you know what I've been doing for the past three months? Studying the records of fires since the founding of my company. The inclination of the house, the direction of the wind that night, the force of the explosion, the places in the bathroom where the fire spread, everything indicates that that hell would not have gone into Domenica's room! The fire would have destroyed one side of the house, it would not have turned around and gone backward. You had to light it again from the garage under her room!"

I looked at him. He saw from my eyes that I was letting myself be persuaded. He had grabbed me by the shoulder. I pulled away.

"Get out of the way or I'll run you down!"

"And then burn your car the way you burned the other one? Well this time, take my advice: don't get carried away, don't lose your head, *take it easy when you make a hole in your gas tank!* If you look carefully, you can tell."

I drove away. He stumbled against the back fender of the Fiat and lost his balance. I heard Mme. Yvette shrieking.

I drove too badly since my operation to go fast. I saw night fall and the lights of La Ciotat come on along the

ge Reppo left work at five o'clock as he had
mer, I would not find him. And he must not

s not at the post office. I called Florence again.
I could not reach Jeanne. At the wheel of the car again,
it was dark and cold, I did not even have the courage to
put the top down.

I drove around La Ciotat a while, as if I hoped to see
Serge Reppo, and indeed part of me hoped I would. The
other part thought only of Micky, whom I was or was
not, and of Jeanne. She could not be deceived, she could
not deceive me. Serge was lying, Micky had known nothing. I was Do and I had killed for nothing, for an inheritance that I had lost, but which would have been given
to me without a murder. I need only have waited. It was
funny. It was laughable. Why wasn't I laughing?

I drove back toward Cap Cadet. In the distance, I
saw several cars with their headlights on in front of the
house: the police. I stopped on the side of the road. I
tried to reason with myself, to make plans, to go over
that fire in my mind one more time.

That was funny too. For three months I had been
searching, digging. Like this gallant little insurance
salesman, I was conducting an investigation too, but I
had been more fortunate than he: in this business which
intrigued him so much, everything led to me. I was the
detective, the murderer, the victim, and the witness, all
at once. What had really happened no one would discover, no one but a little monk with short hair, tonight,
tomorrow, or ever.

I went toward the house on foot. Surrounded by the
black cars of those who had invaded the ground floor was
Jeanne's white car with its hood down, her bag in the

back, a scarf left behind on the front seat. She was here. . . .

I walked away slowly with my coat pulled tightly about me, feeling through my glove the shape of Micky's revolver in my pocket. I went to the beach. Serge was not there. I went back up to the road. He was not there. I got into my car again and returned to La Ciotat.

I found him an hour later in the terrace of a café with a girl with red hair. When he saw me get out of the car he looked around, annoyed at the meeting. I went toward him, and he rose. He even took two steps toward me under the lamps, his last two catlike steps. I fired at him at five yards, missed, and kept walking toward him, discharging my little revolver. He fell forward, head first onto the pavement at the edge of the sidewalk. After the fourth shot I pulled the trigger twice to no effect. It did not matter, I knew he was dead.

There were screams, the sound of running. I got back into the Fiat. I threw the car into gear amid a stream of people which closed around me. They made way for the car. I said to myself, Now they won't be able to bother Jeanne any more, she'll take me in her arms, she'll rock me to sleep, I'll ask nothing but that she continue to love me. My headlights scattered the vultures, who ran in all directions.

In the dining room of the villa Jeanne was standing with her back to a wall: calm, only a little paler than usual, waiting.

She was the first to see me appear at the top of the steps. Her face, suddenly contorted, relieved, and dismayed all at once, blinded me to all the rest. It was not until much later, when they separated me from her, that

I became aware of the presence of the others: Mme. Yvette crying into her apron, Gabriel, two policemen in uniform, three in plain clothes, and one of the men I had seen that morning in front of the garage.

She told me that they were accusing me of the murder of Domenica Loi, that they were going to take me away and indict me, but that it was absurd: I was to have confidence in her, I knew she would not let them hurt me.

"I know, Jeanne."

"Nothing will happen to you. Nothing can. They will try to influence you, but don't listen to anyone."

"I will listen to you."

They pulled me away. Jeanne asked whether we could go up together and pack a bag. A detective with a Marseille accent said that he would come with us. He stayed in the hall. Jeanne closed the door of my room and leaned against it. She began to cry while she was looking at me.

"Tell me who I am, Jeanne."

She shook her head, her eyes full of tears, and said that she did not know, I was her little girl, she no longer knew. It no longer mattered.

"You knew Micky too well to make a mistake. You know me . . . You knew her well, didn't you?"

She shook her head over and over, saying no, no, it was the truth, she did not know her, she was the one who had known her least for the last four years. Micky had avoided her like the plague, she no longer knew her.

"What happened four years ago?"

She cried and cried, held me against her, saying nothing, nothing, nothing happened, nothing, only a kiss, nothing more, just a kiss, but she didn't understand, she didn't understand, she couldn't stand me to come near her, she didn't understand.

She pushed me away roughly, wiping her eyes with the back of her hand, and packed a bag. I went and sat on the bed beside her.

"I'm putting in three sweaters," she told me, calmer. "You'll tell me whatever you need."

"Micky knew, Jeanne."

She shook her head, saying please, please, she knew nothing, you wouldn't be here if she had known. You're the one who would have died.

"Why did you want to kill her?" I asked her more softly, taking her arm. "For the money?"

She shook her head, saying no, no, I couldn't stand it any more, I didn't give a damn for the money, don't talk, please.

I gave up. I laid my cheek on her hand. She let it stay there. She arranged my clothes in the bag with one hand. She had stopped crying.

"I will have had only you, after all," I told her. "Not the inheritance, not the world just before sleep; only you."

"What do you mean, 'the world just before sleep'?"

"You told me about it yourself: the stories I used to tell myself when I worked for the bank."

They asked me questions. They shut me up in a hospital room. Once again my life was divided into the darkness of sleep and the harsh glare of the light when they opened the door to the yard for my walk.

I saw Jeanne twice through a grating in the visiting room. I did not torment her with more questions. She had been pale and depressed since she had been informed of the murder of the little post office employee. She had understood many things that had happened in her absence, and even the smile she tried to put on for my benefit was gone.

They had examined what was left of the MG in an automobile graveyard in La Ciotat, and gone into the life of Serge Reppo. They had discovered traces of deliberate puncturing on a broken gasoline tank, but no conclusive evidence of murder. In the end I realized that the blackmailer was bluffing, that there was no record for the receipt of telegrams. He must have had Micky sign a meaningless piece of paper.

I had killed Serge Reppo to prevent him from talking about Jeanne's role, but even my second murder was for nothing. It was she who talked, after scraping together what money we still had to arrange for our defense.

I confessed when I learned that Jeanne had given herself up. I was indicted, but so was she. I saw her for a few seconds as I was leaving the office of the examining magistrate. We met in the doorway.

"Leave it to me, will you?" she said. "You just be nice and think carefully."

She touched my hair and said it had grown out nicely. She told me I was going to be taken to Italy for additional investigation.

"Be a good Micky," she added. "Be as I've taught you to be."

She told everything they wanted to know and more, but no one ever knew that she had made a pact with Domenica Loi. I knew why: if I said nothing about it, if I was Micky, my punishment would be lighter. She was my governess, so she would be the real culprit.

When darkness returns long hours stretch before me, hours in which to think.

Sometimes I am sure I am Michele Isola. I learn that I am disinherited, that Domenica Loi and Jeanne are plotting my death. At first I decide to frustrate their plans but then, when I see them together at close range I change my mind, I adopt their plan in my own interest, and I kill Domenica in order to take her place.

Sometimes I take Do's place for the inheritance, of which an embittered godmother unjustly deprived me when the end drew near. Sometimes I do it in order to recover I know not what lost affection, Jeanne's. Sometimes to be revenged, sometimes to begin again, sometimes to keep on hurting, sometimes to console. And again, sometimes—closest the truth, no doubt—for all these reasons combined: to retain my fortune and to be someone else for Jeanne.

There are also moments in the night when I become Domenica again. Serge Reppo lied, Micky knew nothing. I killed her, but since the fire did not spread to the bedroom, I lighted another fire in the garage. And without knowing it, I took the place of the very girl who then had a motive for murder.

Whether I am Domenica or Michele, I let myself be trapped at the last minute in the burning room. It is on the second floor, before the window, that I hold the flaming nightgown in my hands, cover my face with it, and bite it in my pain, for charred bits will be found in my mouth. I fall out the window onto the front steps. Neighbors rush up. Jeanne bends over me and since I must of necessity be Do, she recognizes Do in my blackened body, my face without hair or skin.

Then the great burst of light of the clinic. I am the third girl. I have done nothing, planned nothing, I no longer want to be either of the other two. I am myself. Beyond that, death will know her children.

They take care of me. They ask me questions. I speak as little as possible. At the preliminary examination, with my lawyers, with the psychiatrists to whom I am turned over every afternoon, I say nothing or I do not remember. I answer to the name of Michele Isola and I let Jeanne manage our fortunes as she wishes.

Even the malicious irony of Godmother Midola no longer touches me: the will provides for a monthly income for Micky of which Domenica would have been in charge, an income representing the exact salary of the former bank employee.

Micky . . . Two hundred strokes of the hairbrush every day. A cigarette lighted, and immediately put out. Micky falling asleep like a doll. Micky crying in her sleep . . . Am I Micky or Domenica? I no longer know.

What if Serge Reppo had lied to me in the garage, what if he had made up everything after the fact when he read the papers and remembered a telegram? Everything: his meeting with Micky on the beach, the late date at the *tabac* in Les Lecques, the spying she was supposed to have hired him to do before the murder . . . then I am Do, everything has taken place as we had foreseen with Jeanne. Gabriel destroyed his former mistress in his obstinate determination to avenge her, and I destroyed myself by taking Micky's place when she alone had something to gain from the murder.

Domenica or Micky?

If Serge Reppo did not lie, it is Jeanne who was deceived the night of the fire, who is still deceived and always will be. I am Micky and she does not know it.

She does not know it.

She does not know it.

Or, she has known it from the first moment, when I had no hair, no skin, no memories.

I am mad.

Jeanne knows.

Jeanne has known all along.

Because it explains everything. Since I opened my eyes under the white light, Jeanne is *the only one* to have taken me for Do. Everyone I have met, even my lover, even my father, has taken me for Micky. Because *I am Micky*.

Serge Reppo did not lie.

Together Jeanne and Do devised the plot to murder me. I found out what they were planning to do. I killed Do in order to become her, because a cantankerous godmother informed me of the change in the will.

And Jeanne was never deceived. She saw the night of the fire that her plan had miscarried.

She knew I was Micky, but she said nothing. Why?

I made a mistake on the hotel register because before the fire I had taught myself to be Do. I have never been Do. Not for Jeanne, not for anyone.

Why did Jeanne say nothing?

The days pass.

I am alone. Alone to search. Alone to try to understand.

If I am Micky, I know why Jeanne tried to kill me. I

believe I know why, after that, she pretended, in spite of everything, that I was her accomplice. She did not give a damn for the money, no, you must believe me.

If I am Domenica, there is nothing left for me.

In the yard, when it is time for my walk, I try to catch sight of my reflection in a window. It is cold. I am always cold. Micky, too, must always have been cold. Of the two sisters neither of whom I want to be, it is with her that I identify most easily. Was Domenica cold, cold all over, cold with greed and resentment as she prowled under the windows of her victim, the girl with the long hair?

Darkness returns. The matron shuts me again into a cell inhabited by three ghosts. I am in my bed, just as I was on the first night at the clinic. I reassure myself; again tonight I can be whoever I want to be.

Micky, who was loved so much that someone wanted to kill her? Or the other one?

Even when I am Domenica, I accept myself. I remember that they are going to take me far away for a day, a week, or more, and that everything will not be denied me after all: I am going to see Italy.

The prisoner regained her memory one afternoon in January, two weeks after her return from Florence, while looking at a glass of water which she was about to drink. The glass fell to the ground but, God alone knows why, did not break.

Tried the same year at the court at Aix-en-Provence, she was acquitted of the murder of Serge Reppo on account of her mental state at the time of the crime. She was sentenced to ten years of solitary confinement for aiding and abetting Jeanne Murneau in the murder of Domenica Loi.

She appeared very withdrawn at the trial, most of the time letting her former governess answer the questions which were addressed to them jointly.

As she listened to the verdict, she paled a little and raised a white-gloved hand to her mouth. Sentenced to thirty years of the same punishment, Jeanne Murneau, by force of habit, gently lowered her friend's arm and said a few words to her in Italian.

To the gendarme who escorted her from the room, the girl seemed calmer. She guessed that he had served in Algeria. She told him the name of the cologne he used. She had once known a boy who used to douse his head with it. One summer night in a car he had told her the name, something sentimental and military, almost as nauseating as its smell: Trap for Cinderella.

ABSORBING NOVELS

☐ **PICTURING THE WRECK** *A novel* **by Dani Shapiro.** Solomon Grossman is the shattered survivor of two devastating events: the Holocaust and an intensely passionate affair with a beautiful young patient. He endlessly relives his loss of parents, loss of control, and loss of wife and son in a bitter divorce. Then he learns about the wherabouts of his son and what follows is an unforgettable exploration and illumination of the vast gamble that is love. "Powerful, beautifully written."—Tim O'Brien   (277698—$10.95)

☐ **LOUISIANA POWER & LIGHT by John Dufresne.** In this hilarious and highly original novel, the last survivor of the sorry Fontana familial line, Billy Wayne Fontana, strikes out on the rocky road called life and takes us all on a wild, hair-raising ride through the Louisiana backwaters. "Both raucous and wise, it lures us into introspection with humor, and amid guffaws brings home serious truths about faith and heritage, chance and genealogy."—*Chicago Tribune*
                    (275024—$11.95)

☐ **GOODBYE TO THE BUTTERMILK SKY by Julia Oliver.** When twenty-year-old Callie Tatum saw the man from Birmingham coming up the road to the farmhouse, she knew she shouldn't talk to him. Her husband was at the mill. Only her invalid father-in-law and her baby daughter were home, and Callie had no business socializing with a stranger . . . or beginning an affair. "A compelling novel of illicit love against a steamier background."—*Anniston Star*
                    (274257—$10.95)

☐ **TUSCALOOSA by W. Glasgow Phillips.** In the simmering heat of 1972 Tuscaloosa, 22-year-old Billy Mitchell returns from college to live and work on the grounds of the mental institution run by his psychiatrist father. But soon he's overwhelmed by memories of his mother's disappearance years before and his growing passion for one of his father's inmates. "A strong, moving narrative . . . subtle and lyrical . . . draws the reader in with his classical Southern voice while eloquently questioning some of society's labels and prejudices."
—*St. Louis Post-Dispatch*   (274397—$10.95)

☐ **THERAPY by Steven Schwartz.** In this extraordinary and deeply affecting tale of lives that crisscross in and out of therapy, the author draws us achingly close to his characters. An intimate, absorbing novel about hope and hopelessness, about the endless ways in which we can hurt and heal one another, and about the light and dark places in the human heart. "A supreme literary gift . . . triumphs spiritually, intellectually, humanly."—Bret Lott, author of *Reed's Beach*   (274311—$12.95)

Prices slightly higher in Canada.

MODERN CLASSICS

☐ **THE ARMIES OF THE NIGHT** *History as a Novel/The Novel as History.*
**Winner of the Pulitzer Prize and the National Book Award. by Norman
Mailer.** The time is October 21, 1967. The place is Washington, D.C. Intellectuals
and hippies, clergymen and cops, poets and army MPs, crowd the pages of this
book in which facts are fused with techniques of fiction to create the nerve-end
reality of experiential truth. (272793—$12.95)

☐ **THE THIRD POLICEMAN by Flann O'Brien.** Here is the most surreal, fantastic
and imaginative murder comedy ever created, from one of Ireland's most celebrated authors. "Astonishingly inventive . . . to read Flann O'Brien for the first time
is to be plunged into joy."—Bob Moore (259126—$12.95)

☐ **UNDER THE VOLCANO by Malcolm Lowry.** Set in Quahnahuac, Mexico,
against the backdrop of conflicted Europe during the Spanish Civil War, it is a gripping novel of terror and of a man's compulsive alienation from the world and those
who love him. "One of the towering novels of this century."—*The New York Times*
(255953—$12.95)

☐ **1984 by George Orwell.** The world of **1984** is one in which eternal warfare is
the price of bleak prosperity, in which the Party keeps itself in power by complete
control over man's actions and his thoughts. As the lovers Winston Smith and Julia
learn when they try to evade the Thought Police and join the underground opposi-
tion, the Party can smash the last impulse of love, the last flicker of individuality.
(262933—$11.95)

☐ **ANSWERED PRAYERS by Truman Capote.** For years the celebrity set waited
nervously for the publication of this scandalous exposé. For years, the public
eagerly awaited its revelations. The narrator is P.B. Jones, a bisexual hustler. The
heroine is Kate McCloud, the most desired woman in the jet-set world. Between
them they see, do, and tell—everything. "A gift from an unbridled genius!"—*Los
Angeles Times Book Review* (264839—$11.95)

Prices slightly higher in Canada.

Visa and Mastercard holders can order Plume, Meridian, and Dutton books by calling
1-800-253-6476.
They are also available at your local bookstore. Allow 4-6 weeks for delivery.
This offer is subject to change without notice.